k

Crowboy

Crowboy

David Calcutt

OXFORD
UNIVERSITY PRESS

Crowboy was written with assistance from
Arts Council England

OXFORD
UNIVERSITY PRESS

Great Clarendon Street, Oxford OX2 6DP
Oxford University Press is a department of the University of Oxford.
It furthers the University's objective of excellence in research, scholarship,
and education by publishing worldwide in

Oxford   New York

Auckland   Cape Town   Dar es Salaam   Hong Kong   Karachi
Kuala Lumpur   Madrid   Melbourne   Mexico City   Nairobi
New Delhi   Shanghai   Taipei   Toronto

With offices in

Argentina   Austria   Brazil   Chile   Czech Republic   France   Greece
Guatemala   Hungary   Italy   Japan   Poland   Portugal   Singapore
South Korea   Switzerland   Thailand   Turkey   Ukraine   Vietnam

Oxford is a registered trade mark of Oxford University Press
in the UK and in certain other countries

British Library Cataloguing in Publication Data

Data available

ISBN: 978-0-19-272749-7

1 3 5 7 9 10 8 6 4 2

Typeset in Berling Roman by TnQ Books and Journals Pvt. Ltd.,
Chennai, India

Printed in Great Britain by Cox and Wyman Ltd, Reading, Berkshire

Paper used in the production of this book is a natural,
recyclable product made from wood grown in sustainable forests.
The manufacturing process conforms to the environmental
regulations of the country of origion.

Part One

Orf

So I'm outside the city one evening on me usual rounds, sorting through the leftovers and picking me way through the day's dead. Not that there's much to be took. The best of the fighting's over now. That all happened in the first few weeks after the soldiers come, and what with the city having took a good battering and the best of its people dead or run off, everybody's got themselves settled down now to a good long siege. That's how it always happens. And it can go on like this for weeks or months. The longest I've known was almost a year. But it always ends up the same way. The army has a sudden push, the soldiers break in, they go tearing through the place setting everything on fire and killing anything that moves, and then they're off and away again to the next place. I usually try to be off and on me way meself before that happens. It's a risky business, though, and I've come close to getting caught up in it a few times.

Anyway, like I'm saying, I'm outside and I'm doing me rounds and if pickings ain't good they ain't none too bad neither. I can usually find something of currency—

a boot, maybe, or a buckle off a belt, sometimes a helmet that's been overlooked. There's always shrapnel to be picked up, of course, and empty shell-cases. They ain't much in themselves but they can add up over time, and there's always somebody inside willing to trade something for them.

But this evening I'm in luck as how earlier on there's been a bit of a skirmish out here. Seems a gang of them inside got theirselves all worked and fired up and went out on some kind of a raiding party. Suicide mission more like. Far as I can tell there weren't none of them made it back. Bad news for them, good news for me, on two counts. First, one gang less, and second, I get meself some rich pickings.

I gather up about as much as I can carry and then sit meself down against a piece of broken wall to have a bit of a rest before I go back inside. The sun's going down over the mountains and it's still warm, but I know that as soon as it's gone it'll get cold and I want to be inside and snuggled in front of me fire before that happens.

There's a tree nearby. Got no leaves on it, all thin and twisted and burned black. And it's while I'm sitting there not thinking about much in particular that I see there's something hanging from one of the branches. Hanging and swaying and twisting round in the breeze. Well, I'm the kind of bloke got to know what a thing is and can't let it rest till he does, so I gets up and goes to have a closer look and I see that it's a dead crow.

It looks like it's been dead a while, hardly more than a few feathers stuck to scraps of skin and bone. Its feet have been fastened together with a nail, and there's a piece of wire looped through its eyesockets and tied to the branch. I wonder why somebody should go to the trouble of killing a crow and hanging it from a tree like that. But that's the old me, the one that was around before the war started. I suppose there ain't many left like me can remember that far back. I've seen enough since to know that at the right time and in the right place people will do just about anything they can put their minds and hands to. And living in a war's just the right time and place. So no need to wonder.

I don't know why that dead crow should take me like it does though. There's something about it, the way it's just dangling there, so long dead it don't seem to ever have had much to do with being alive. Like being alive don't have no real connection with what's hanging up there. And thinking that I start to get the feeling that being alive ain't got much connection with me neither, how I'm just a few scraps meself all tied with string and walking around but not really living. Well, that ain't a nice thought to have when the sun's setting and the dark and the cold's coming on, so I stamp me feet to try and shake off the mood, and I'm turning round to go back inside when I see them.

They're coming across the plain, with the mountains behind them, and it's like the mountains are on fire, and they're walking out of the flames of that fire. Just shadows at first, little stick-figures coming towards the city, with the earth and the sky burning all around them. And at first I think there's two of them, and then I think there's three, but with the light in me eyes I can't be sure. But one thing I am sure of is that they ain't just coming here. They're coming here for a reason, and it scares me, and I want to get away. But I know I can't, I'll have to stay, because I know I'm a part of that reason as well.

Joey

we walk together and he walks ahead leading us though I know only I can see him and sometimes it's difficult even for me   in the day he is a shimmering of light the way you see it in a pool or a stream sometimes and it sparkles and flashes and is very beautiful   at night sometimes only a faint mist like the mist you see around the moon on a clear night but much closer   sometimes so close I can almost touch him   I have tried to tell her but I can't find the words to say it and I think maybe there are no words only what you can see and this makes me sad because I would like her to know that he is with us   guiding us protecting us   she was chosen as well she has her part to play whatever it is   maybe I will have to find a way to show her or make a sign we are near the place now and he is a deep red his hair and his wings are flames and I know that soon it will be revealed to me the purpose   so we walk on   me and she together   he in front leading   the three of us

Orf

There are two of them, a boy and a girl, and by the looks
of them they've been through it, and come a long way.
Ragged and dirty and starved-looking, but that ain't
nothing new. The girl don't look to be that old, and the
boy maybe even younger, only there's something about
him somehow seems a lot older, something in his eyes.
Like when he's looking at something he ain't looking at it
but looking at something inside it or way beyond it. The
same when he looks at me. It don't make me feel easy.

He seems to lose interest pretty quick, though, and turns
away, while the girl comes walking up to me and starts
talking straight out, and our conversation goes something
like this.

'You from the city?'

'Depends what you mean.'

'I mean do you live there?'

'Not exactly. I'm kind of staying there for the time
being. Till I reckon it's time to move on.'

'What's the best way in?'

'There ain't no way in. No way in and no way out. It's
under siege or hadn't you noticed?'

'You're out.'

'I come and go as I please.'

'Tell us how to get in.'

'What you want to get in for?'

'We just do. Tell us.'

'Who are you, anyway? Where'd you come from?'

'Over that way.'

'From the mountains?'

'The other side.'

'That's a long way to travel. Hard road as well.'

'It hasn't been easy.'

'And how'd you get through?'

'Get through?'

'Like I've already said, the city's under siege. Has been for months. There's soldiers dug in all the way round. From the mountains down to the river. So how'd you get through them?'

That brings her up sharp and there's this puzzled look suddenly comes across her face, like she hadn't even thought about it till now. She looks to the boy, but he ain't no help, he's sitting by the tree and messing about with something on the ground and don't take no notice. Then she looks out to the mountains where they come from like she's trying to remember something, but gives up on that and shakes her head and looks back at me and shrugs and says, 'I don't know. Maybe they just didn't see us.'

And it ain't until a while after that it strikes me as being in any way strange her saying that.

Right now she's on at me again asking if I can show them a way into the city. And looking at her and him squatting down there in the dust under the tree, I know that if they do go in there they're going to come in for trouble and unpleasantness of every kind on account of how things have pretty much broken down and it's only the real tough and the real sharp manage to stay alive. And they don't look neither tough nor sharp. So I tell her that if they've got any sense left at all they'll turn round and go back to the mountains. They'll be better off there than in the city.

'It's pretty bad in there,' I say, 'and it's going to get worse. It's only a matter of time before the soldiers break in, and you can guess what'll happen then.'

'I don't need to guess,' she says. 'I know. I've seen it.'

And by the look on her face and in her eyes I can see that she has. And I can see as well that nothing I say'll change her mind about wanting to get in there, though what for and why I can't imagine. But what their business might be ain't no concern of mine. I got enough on me plate looking after me own. And if I don't show them how to get in, they'll find some other way, so I might as well as not. Like I said, it ain't got nothing to do with me.

So I tell her all right, I'll show them how to get in, and she turns to the boy and says, 'Come on, Joey. He's going to show us the way in.'

He looks up at her like it don't come as no surprise to him, like he was just waiting for her to say it, then he stands and comes over to me and holds out something in one of his hands. It's a piece of twisted wire, I can see that right enough, but like a fool I says, 'What's that?'

And he speaks, the first time he's said anything, and I won't forget the sound of his voice in a long time.

'There was a bird in a cage. But now the cage is broken and the bird's free.'

He drops the wire on the ground and turns away like he's forgot all about it and me. And then it hits me where I've seen that wire before, and I look towards the tree and sure enough the wire ain't there no more, nor the dead crow that was hanging from it. But though the wire's laying in the dust there at me feet, there ain't no sign of that dead crow anywhere. Probably got it stuffed in his coat or one of his pockets, I thinks to meself. Or ate it. He looks hungry enough and crazy enough. But even though I'm just thinking it I know it's a cheap joke and I feel a bit ashamed of meself for it. It just annoys me that the crow's gone and I didn't see it go nor what he done with it and I don't like to think I'm being made a fool of.

'Are we going then?' the girl says to me, and I nod and tell her just a minute, and get me takings together and put them in me bag and sling it over me shoulder and say, 'Right then. Follow me.'

Then I take them along the wall to the place where there's a hole covered over with a tangle of dead bushes, and I tell her as how it leads down to an old tunnel that runs under the city a little way and comes up by a canal, and that's how I get in and out, and if they want to follow me they can.

'But you'll have to watch out,' I tell them. 'It's full of rats and other godless creatures, and it don't smell too good neither.'

'That's OK,' says the girl. 'We've been through worse.'

Yes, I says to meself, no doubt you have. But it ain't half as bad as what you'll go through once you get inside. But I don't say nothing about that to them. I just crawl through and there's the steps and I go down into tunnel and they come after and I lead them through the dark and the stink into the city.

Geeks: Schyte

We're on lookout in one of the old buildings right on the edge of our territory and it ain't fair cos this is the third night in a row I been on lookout and it's freezing and I ain't got no coat. Fig has, all right, but her won't share it with me cos her's a selfish cow is what her is and I don't mind telling her so neither and I do but her don't take no notice. It's cold like I ain't never knowed it cold before and there her is sat snuggled up in her coat and here's me with me arse and ballocks freezing off and I'm right pissed off about it though if I tried to piss I couldn't it'd freeze before it hit the ground. So I ask her again, Hey, Fig, I say to her, lend us your coat just for ten minutes, go on. And her says to me, No, and I say to her, Five minutes then, and her says, Not ten minutes not five minutes not ten seconds, it's my coat and I'm keeping it so give up asking and shut your fat trap.

Well, that ain't very friendly is it, we're supposed to be sisters and brothers all one family, that's how Akh puts it, but there ain't no point arguing with her and anyhow actions speak louder than words, so I starts walking up and down and stomping me feet and flapping me arms about hoping her'll take pity on me, but all her says is, What you doing there, Schyte, think you're a bird or summat trying to fly away, and I say, No, I'm trying to keep warm, stupid. You're the stupid one, her says, making all that noise, do you want to give us away, or summat? So I say to her that if I could get warm I wouldn't have to stomp up and down, would I, so why don't you let me share your coat if you won't lend it to me, it's a big coat and there's plenty of room inside for the two of us. And I go up to her and I say, How about it, Fig, let me get in there with you and we can snuggle up together. And her says to me, Go and snuggle up on your own, Schyte, her says, you ain't snuggling in here with me, now back off or you'll eat iron.

So I give up any hope a getting warm and go across to the window and take a look out. It's all broke down buildings out there from the shelling when the army first come, some of them just walls standing on their own, there ain't nobody lives in them now, only rats and a few stray cats and dogs that ain't been ate. It's a clear night and the moon must be up cos it's all lit up bright out there and frosty and all I can see it sparkling off the streets. Off the smashed up houses and rusty pipes and broken windows and the rubbish in the streets what nobody can put a name to no more. Bits and pieces of people's lives. And all cos of this war what nobody can remember no more what it's about if ever they ever knowed in the first place.

It's got its good side though, ain't it, cos if it hadn't been for the war coming here there wouldn't be no gangs to belong to and no Geeks and being part of the Geeks is the best thing's ever happened to me in my life. Better than me life like it was before. That wasn't no kind a life at all.

I'm still looking out of the window when Fig says, What was that? What was what, I say to her, and her says, That noise, and I say, I didn't hear no noise, which I didn't, cos I'd've said if I had, wouldn't I? I heard summat, her says, and I ask her what and her says her don't know, just some kind of noise definite, maybe somebody's coming. There ain't nobody coming, I says, I been looking out the window and there ain't nobody out there, then the door busts open and in they come.

It's Troggs, four of them, Lex, Ell, Uba, and Yass, and they're armed, chains, crowbars, piping, the lot. Fig's up on her feet straight off with her weapon, but her can see it ain't no good trying to make a fight of it, they've got us outnumbered good and proper. Lex knows it, and all, and he ain't going to make no quick work of it, he's going to take his time and enjoy himself, he's like that, Lex, a right nasty piece a work. He signals to the others to hold back and stands all easy-like and grinning and says, Best drop your weapon, Fig, if you know what's good for yourself. It won't do you no good, one Geek against four Troggs. Then Uba pipes up saying, Poor little Figgy-wig, out here all on her ownsome, and nobody to take care of her. They ain't looked at me yet, and it's like they ain't even noticed I'm there, which is a bit funny cos I'm standing right in front of them.

Course, that's all part of the joke, ain't it, cos right after Ell holds her nose and pulls a face and says, What's that stink, and starts into coughing and choking and holding her throat, and the others all join in making noises, and Yass says, Smells like summat's died in here, what is it, a dead dog you was going to have for your supper? Then Uba looks at me like he's only just seen me and says, It ain't no dead dog, it's just Schyte, summat's died in his gut, Schyte by name and Schyte by nature, which is a really good joke, ain't it, like I ain't never heard it before.

They're all having a good laugh about it except me, even Fig her starts to laugh but as soon as her does Lex stops and asks her what's so funny and the others stop laughing and all and suddenly it's got serious and I can tell it won't be long before the trouble starts. I'm wondering if I can slide out through the window, so I start edging towards it slow while Lex is getting closer to Fig and jabbing his finger at her, saying over and over, What's funny, what is there to laugh at, some kind of joke is there, I don't see nothing much funny and you won't neither in a bit when I've smashed your teeth in, and other stuff like that. I'm getting closer to the window when Fig says, What you want here, Lex, what you doing here, this ain't your territory, it's our'n. Her's got guts, I have to admit it, coming back like that with the four of them there, and it makes sure that they're all looking at her and not at me as I get even closer to the window.

Next thing Lex takes a step in closer to Fig and says, Your territory is it, that's where you're wrong, cos it's ours now we're claiming it. Then he brings his knee up sharp into Fig's gut and her doubles up and drops down onto her knees gasping, and I start to sneak me leg out the window when Ell sees me and yells out and Uba makes a grab at me and at the same time I can see Lex raising his crowbar over Fig's head but before Uba can take hold of me or Lex can bring his crowbar down here's Akh in at the door and swinging Lex round and knocking the crowbar out of his hand, and here's Rok and Jax and Dis in behind him saving the day like shining angels of mercy.

Lost your way, ain't you, Lex, says Akh, this is Geek territory, you're trespassing, and Lex stares back at him and says, No, we just come for what's our'n. And what might that be, says Dis. You know what, says Lex, our goods what you stole. You calling us thieves, says Rok, you'll pay for that. Pay good and proper, says Jax, let's do them. Yeah, like they done to Fig, says Rok, only worse. And they're about to lay into them when Akh holds up his hand and says, Ease up, lads, not now and not here. Then he says to Lex again, he says, Go and tell Ekt that if he wants anything he can come and fight for it hisself, fair and square. If he's got the guts for it, puts in Rok, and Lex says, He's got the guts all right, and Jax comes back with, Make sure he brings them, then, so's we can spill them for him. Lex don't say nothing for a bit, then, he just stands there staring at Akh and the others like he's thinking of something really clever to say, but before he can, Dis says to him, What you waiting for, Lex? Sod off out of it before it's your guts as gets spilled. So Lex picks up his weapon and gives the nods to Ell and Uba and Yass and they make for the door, but just before they go he turns and says, We're going but we'll be back, don't you worry about that, you'll see us coming but you won't be seeing nothing once we've done.

After they've gone Dis helps Fig up to her feet and they're talking about what we're gonna do to the Troggs and how pretty soon there won't be no more Troggs only Geeks to run the whole territory, and it's only then I realize I've still got me leg half out the window, and just before I can get it back in Jax turns to me and he says, What you doing, Schyte, coming or going. And before I can say anything Fig ups and says as how soon as the Troggs come I was sneaking off out of it and leaving her to face them on her own, which is a mean thing to say, specially as what I was doing was going to get help and I would've got it and all if Akh and the others hadn't turned up when they did. It ain't no use trying to tell her though nor the others, and the next thing I know is Akh's told me to stay on lookout on me own cos Fig ain't in no fit state and the rest am needed for a council of war and we can't leave nobody on lookout can we so as I'm already here it might as well be me.

Well, I got plenty to say about that only it ain't the right time just now, I'll wait till after we've give them Troggs a thrashing tomorrow, then I'll have something to say about it, you bet. And I'll have something to say to Fig and all cos as they're going I ask her if I can borrow her coat seeing as how her's going back to camp and I've got need of it, but her won't, will her, I might've knowed it, so here I am now on lookout on me own and the whole ballock-freezing night in front a me and no coat nor nothing and like I said before it ain't fair.

Mal

I don't know what we're doing here.

We've stopped to rest by the side of the canal. We've been going for a while, but I think we're still a long way from the centre of the city. Still in the outskirts. All around us are the ruins of buildings—old factories and warehouses, that look like they've been empty a long time. Long before the soldiers came, probably. It feels as if the whole area's been derelict for years. There's nothing moving, no sound, no sign of life. Except us. Me and Joey. And the sooner we move on from here the better.

There's something I don't like about this place. It's too still, too quiet. As if there is something else here, hidden, watching us from the shadows, waiting to pounce.

The old man said it was dangerous.

After he brought us up out of the sewer he took us first of all to where he camped. It was a kind of a recess in the side of a bridge over the canal. Not what you'd call comfortable. Water dripping from the ceiling and trickling down the walls. Cold. Cramped. And a bad smell. The old man said it didn't matter to him, though. He'd camped in worse. And he reckoned he'd be moving on soon.

'Just as soon as the city falls,' he said.

I asked him when he thought that would be and he said not long. He'd been in quite a few besieged cities and he could tell when things were getting near the end. He gave me a look then, and I thought he was going to ask me why we'd come here. He didn't though, and I was glad about it. I wouldn't've known what to say.

Because I don't know. Only Joey knows that and he's not telling.

The place where the old man was camped was full of stuff. Junk. Scraps. Bits and pieces, odds and ends. Things he'd picked up from inside and outside the city. It wasn't arranged in any order, just dumped anyhow all over the place so that you couldn't move anywhere without having to step over or squeeze your way past something. In one corner there was a pile of old shoes and boots.

'That's the best currency,' he said. 'Shoes. There's always somebody on the lookout for shoes, any kind, any size, even if they got no soles in them. It changes from city to city,' he went on. 'The last place I was in it was hats. Hats, caps, scarves, anything like that. I made myself a pretty good collection before the end. A rich man, I was, in that city. I suppose you might say I'm pretty well-off here, as well, seeing as shoes are currency and I've got this lot. It changes, though, like I said. City to city. It depends what they put a value on.

It was like that in my city too. But I don't like to think about it. I don't like to think much about what happened there.

But thinking about that old man, now, I reckon he was a bit crazy. Maybe more than a bit. Following the war around from city to city, living there for a while until the city fell, then moving on. It doesn't seem to make any sense. Mind you, what me and Joey are doing makes even less sense. All that time we spent crossing the mountains to get away from the war, and now here we are walking straight back into it. And not for any reason I can see.

If there is a reason only Joey can see it. And sometimes it seems to me his eyes are turned the wrong way round.

The old man said he'd been following the war ever since it started. He couldn't have been much older than us. The army burned the town where he lived so he went off to find somewhere else. But as soon as he found somewhere the army arrived and burned that as well. So he went to another town and that got burned too. Everywhere he went, the war came after. So he decided that if he couldn't escape the war, he might as well go along with it, and make some kind of living at the same time. Collecting, trading. The war had taken everything he had, he said, so he felt he might as well take back from it what he could. It was as good a way as any to make a living. And, besides that, he liked collecting things.

'Not just goods,' he said. 'Stories, too. I like collecting stories. And there's plenty of stories happens where the war is.'

Then he said it looked like we had a good story to tell, and I said maybe we had, and maybe I'd tell him if we saw him again.

'You do that,' he said, 'if you make it out of here.'

But from the way he said it, it didn't seem like he thought we would.

I'm not sure we will either. And if we do, what'll become of us? Will we end up like the old man, wandering around from city to city, following the war because the war's the only way of life we know? That doesn't seem like any kind of life to me. But maybe I shouldn't try and think ahead too far into the future. Every time I try to do that, I just see this kind of emptiness, this big, dark empty space waiting for me to walk into it and be lost for ever. Is that where Joey's leading us, into that emptiness? And if he is, why am I following him? Why am I letting him lead the way?

Because. That's why. Because of what happened when I first saw him. Because he's special.

Though there doesn't seem much special about him right now. He's just sitting there hunched up on a pile of bricks looking down into the water. The surface of the canal's frozen and the light from the moon's glittering off the thin ice. But Joey's face is in shadow, and it's only when you see his face that you see he's special.

It was the old man who told us to make our way along the canal. He said it went all the way into the centre of the city, and once we reached there we'd probably be all right. That's where most people lived now and there'd be somebody who'd help us. He said to keep moving and get away from the outskirts as quickly as we could.

'There ain't many people live out here no more,' he said. 'And them that do ain't the kind you want to come across.'

I asked him why he lived out here, if it was so dangerous.

'Nobody bothers with the likes of me,' he said. 'I'm just a crazy old man. But when the end comes, when the army finally breaks through, I'll be first out, won't I?'

Out and on your way, I said to him. Off to the next city.

'That's about it,' he said.

That was the last thing he said to us before we left him and started off along the canal. He didn't watch us go. We've been going about an hour now and we're still in the outskirts. The badlands, the old man called them. Just here, on one side, the canal runs along the top of a bank, and when I look down, as far as I can see there's more of the same—half-tumbled buildings, empty streets, junk and rubble, wasteland. Miles and miles of it. Not a single light burning anywhere. And beyond the wasteland, darkness. That big, dark empty space. Like a throat opened wide and waiting to swallow us. And that's where we're heading. Into that throat.

It's going to take us a long time to get out of here. Maybe we won't reach the centre till daybreak. So I think we'll just rest for a few minutes more and then be on our way again. I'll have to wake Joey. The way he's sitting it looks like he's fallen asleep.

There was no doubt in the old man's mind that the city will fall, and fall soon. I don't doubt it either. And when it happens—well, I've seen it before, and I don't want to see it again. I shouldn't think Joey does either. So I just hope that whatever he's brought us here for, we can be done with it and away again before the soldiers get in.

They don't leave anything standing or anybody living.

Troggs: Nasty, Ik

'You see them?'
 'Yeah.'
 'Who you reckon they are?'
 'I dunno.'
 'What they doing here?'
 'I dunno that either.'
 'I never seen them before.'
 'Nor me.'
 'Must be strangers.'
 'Strangers. Yeah.'
 'What shall we do?'
 'What do you mean?'
 'I mean, what shall we do?'
 'Do about what?'
 'Do about them.'
 'Nothing.'
 'Nothing?'
 'Let's do nothing.'
 'They're on our territory.'
 'Probably just passing through.'
 'They could be Geeks.'

'We'd know them if they was Geeks.'
'New recruits.'
'We'd know if they was.'
'They must be somebody.'
'Strangers. Just passing through.'
'We got to do something.'
'Why?'
'Ekt said.'
'Ekt said if we seen Geeks.'
'What if they're going to the Geeks?'
'I don't reckon they are.'
'But we don't know.'
'Let's just leave them.'
'Let's just not.'
'What you want to do?'
'Take them.'
'Prisoners.'
'Yeah.'
'What for?'
'Cos it's what we're supposed to do.'
'Then what?'
'What you mean?'
'After we've took them prisoner.'
'Take them back to camp.'
'And then what?'
'I dunno. It's up to Ekt.'
'I ain't sure.'
'I am.'

'There's two of them.'

'Two of us. And we're Troggs.'

'All right, then.'

'Yeah?'

'Yeah.'

'Ready?'

'Ready.'

'Right, then.'

Mal

He isn't asleep. He's got a doll. He's found some old broken doll and he's doing something with it. Tying something to it. What is it? I go closer to have a look, see what he's doing.

It's feathers. A couple of black feathers, from a crow or something. And he's tying them to the arms of that broken doll.

Anybody but me would think he was crazy. And even I think he's crazy sometimes. But if he's crazy, what does that make me?

I'm going to ask him what he's doing with those feathers and that doll. Not that I expect any kind of answer that'll make any sense. But I've got to ask him.

'Joey,' I say to him. 'What are you doing?'

He doesn't say anything. Acts like he hasn't heard me. He probably hasn't.

'Joey,' I say again, and this time he looks up. 'What are you doing with that old doll?'

'She wants to fly,' he says. 'I'm giving her wings.'

I might have known it. I could leave it there, or I could ask him what he means, and then we'll get into one of those crazy conversations we have sometimes, which seem to make sense until you listen to what it is you're saying, and then you realize it doesn't make any sense at all.

Once, just before we went into the mountains, we had one of those conversations. It was evening and we were camping among the rocks. We'd been travelling for about two weeks and I was beginning to wonder if we were heading for any place in particular, so I thought I'd ask him. It went something like this.

'Joey, are we going anywhere?'

'Yes,' he said.

'Do you know where?'

'I'll know when we get there.'

'But you don't know right now.'

'It's not clear.'

'So how will you know when we're there?'

'It will be shown.'

I thought about this, then I said, 'If you don't know exactly where it is we're going, how do you know we're going the right way?'

'I follow,' he said.

'You follow.'

'Yes.'

'Follow who? Follow what?'

He didn't say anything for a while. He just looked straight ahead, up towards the mountains. They were very close, lit by the sun as it went down. Everything else was dark around them. In one place it looked like the rock was on fire. That's where he was looking. Then he turned to me and he said, 'The way.'

'The way?'

'I follow the way. You follow, and I follow. We all follow the way.'

He didn't say any more after that.

We all follow the way. It didn't seem to make much sense at the time, but when I thought about it afterwards, and when I think about it now, there seems to be something in it. Something under the words, or inside them. Something you can't really say in words. And if I was to think about it more I might begin to get at it. But I don't like to think about things too much. That's when I start to remember, and there are things I don't want to remember right now.

It's easier just to follow.

He's on his feet now, standing at the edge of the canal. He looks up, then he lifts the doll above his head and moves it slowly backwards and forwards. As if it's flying. Turning, twisting, dipping, rising. Weaving patterns in the air. He closes his eyes and his face is shining in the moonlight. He smiles. Lifts himself up onto his toes, rocking backwards and forwards. I tell him to be careful he doesn't fall into the water, but he doesn't hear. It doesn't matter. I know he won't fall in.

I watch him, watch the doll flying in his upraised

hand, watch the feathers he's tied to its arms fluttering.
I say to him, 'Where'd you get the feathers from, Joey?'

'The bird.'

'What bird?'

'The bird that was in the cage.'

I remember the dead crow on the tree outside the city. How it was there when we got there, and wasn't there when we left. He must've taken it down. But I didn't see him do it, and neither did the old man.

'Where's the bird now?' I ask him.

'Up there.'

He keeps his eyes shut and points upward with his other hand, the one that's not holding the doll.

'There's no bird up there.'

'There is. Look.'

I look where he's pointing. There's a star, cold and bright, bigger than the others around it.

'That's just a star,' I say.

'It's the bird,' he says.

Then he opens his eyes and turns to me.

'It's a star,' I say.

'They're the same thing,' he says.

And he grins, like it's all just some kind of game, and maybe it is. I grin back and say, 'We'd better be moving.'

'No,' he says. He's still grinning. But I stop.

'What do you mean?' I say.

'We stay here,' he says.

'Here?' I say to him. 'What for? There's nothing here.'

'This is the place,' he says, and he walks away from the edge of the canal and sits back on the wall that runs along the top of the bank.

'The place?' I say. 'What place? This is nowhere. We've got to get to the centre. That's what the old man said. He said we'd be safe there.'

Joey just looks at the doll and shakes his head.

'We've got to keep moving,' I say to him. 'There's nothing here.'

Suddenly there's a splash in the water. I look up and see a rat swimming across the canal to the other side. Little glints of light come from the ripples it makes.

'OK,' I say, 'so there's a rat. But there's nothing else.'

'Yes, there is,' he says.

Then there's another noise, coming from behind us this time. A kind of scuffling sound. Joey turns his head, and I turn to look as well. And then—

Troggs: Nasty

There's gonna be a fight.

Us and the Geeks. Soon as the sun rises. I just heard it. Heard Ekt say it. All we got to do now is get ready. Then it'll be time. Won't be long. Then we go and fight the Geeks. About time. Get our own back. And our goods what they took from we. Finish them off and all. Good and proper. Smash their heads, spill their guts, no more Geeks.

Yeah.

I knew there was summat like that brewing. Soon as we got the prisoners we'd took back to camp and there wasn't nobody there only Kazz. I asked her where everybody was and her said they'd gone off to headquarters for a meeting. So I asked her a meeting what about but her didn't know. Her wouldn't. I did though. I had a feeling right then. There wouldn't be no other reason why they was all having a meeting.

It's like I knew there was summat in the air right from when me and Ik started patrol. I felt it, that kind of tingling you get. Makes you edgy, like everything's watching you, and you got to be sharp for what's coming. So when I seen them two by the canal I knew we had to take them. Couldn't help it. Wasn't nothing else to be done. I knew they'd come easy and they did. Give we no trouble. One of them's a bit soft in the head. The other give a bit of lip first off, but I told her to shut it or I'd shut it for her and that worked. It usually does.

They was just the start of it though, like a taster. We got the real thing coming now.

Soon as Kazz said that about a meeting I knew. I knew I had to go and find out. So I said to Ik stay here with these two, you and Kazz watch them and make sure they don't escape. He said OK but I knew he warn't happy about it. He warn't happy about taking them in the first place. I wonder why he's with us sometimes. He ain't much good when it comes to a fight. His heart ain't in it. And if your heart ain't in it you ain't gonna be much good. Lex wants to get rid of him but Ekt won't cos he's Kazz's brother. I think Lex'd like to get rid of Kazz and all but he don't say it. I reckon Kazz scares him like her scares me. I don't mind admitting that. The way her looks at you sometimes. Like summat's woke up inside you and it's crawling around. It ain't nice.

Her was looking at him like that, the one that's soft in the head. Soon as we brought them in. Like he was some kind of freak. Like her warn't no kind of freak herself. Staring and staring like when her goes off into one of them fits her has. I got a bit worried then. I thought her was going to go off on one and I'd have to stay and help Ik with her and not go and find out about the meeting. But her didn't. So I said to Ik you keep your eyes on her like her has on him and they won't get away. Then I left them to it.

It ain't far to headquarters. Down the cut a bit, over the lock, round the side of the old warehouse and there it is. Only I was busting a gut to know what they was talking about and hoping it was what I thought, and it seemed to take for ever. Course I got there in the end. But when I did there was Uba standing guard outside. Not much of a guard, mind. He was chucking stones at one of the buildings over the way. Trying to get them over the wall and in the hole where the roof used to be. Not having much luck.

Uba, I said, and he dropped the stone he was going to throw and turned round.

Who is it, he said.

Who is it? You can see who it is. It's me.

I got to ask, said Uba. Course he has. Tell him to do summat and he does it. He's good at that, following orders. Saves thinking. Mind, he's a good fighter, and all.

I asked him what was going on and he told me. Him and Lex and a couple of the others had a run in with Akh and some other of the Geeks and the end of it was the Geeks offered we a challenge. And that's what they was all meeting to talk about. If we should take them up on it or not.

So what was there to talk about?

Uba shrugged and I left him to carry on throwing stones and missing, and I opened up the doors and dropped down into the cellar. They was there, Ekt, Lex, Yass, and Ell, and they was having some kind of argument. But they stopped when they seen me and Ekt turned to me and said what you doing here, Nasty, why ain't you out on patrol? Really sharp and all and there warn't no call for it. Anyway, I was just going to tell him about the prisoners we'd took when Lex said never mind about that now let's get this business settled.

They started in to arguing again. Lex and Ell was all for taking up the challenge and going out to smash the Geeks. Yass di'n't seem so sure. We should be calling the shots, not them, he said. Let's wait until we'm good and ready. If we ain't ready now, said Lex, we won't never be. Yeah, that's right, said Ell and Lex followed up with, Strike hard, strike fast, and strike now. Maybe you'm right, said Yass, but Ekt's the one to say, Lex, not you. Ekt's boss and he has the word. Let him give it, then, said Lex, and then straight to Ekt, he said, we've been give a challenge, Ekt. We gonna take it or not?

I was just standing back listening to all this, and waiting for Ekt to say something, but he di'n't, he just stood there looking down at the floor like he still warn't sure which way to go with it. He's like that, Ekt, takes a time to make up his mind, but when it's made it's made. I thought maybe I'd help him along, like, and put in a word meself, so I said, Let's give them what they want. Show them we ain't afraid.

I was gonna say more but I never got the chance. Soon as I spoke Ekt turned round to me sharp and said, You saying I'm afraid, am you, Nasty?

That ain't what I was saying, and I started to tell him. But he stepped up real close and it was like he was ready to fix me proper. He dropped his voice quiet and said, you reckon if I say we don't go it's because I'm scared? Eh? Nasty? Is that what you reckon? I didn't say that, I said to him, and he was gonna come back with summat, but then Lex said, he didn't say it but the Geeks will. Ekt's afraid, they'll say. His bottle's lost.

That done the trick. Ekt turned back to Lex and the others and I was off the hook. I ain't scared of nothing nor nobody, said Ekt, and his voice was loud again. If you was all Geeks here I'd take you on. I'd stand me ground nor never shift nor run.

And that's when Lex come in with, So we'm gonna fight them.

And Ekt grinned at him, but it was the kind of grin you give somebody before you smash their face in.

You bet we am, he said.

So that's it. Settled. We'm gonna fight the Geeks. Soon as the sun's up, going across to their territory. They'll be waiting for we. And we'll be ready for them. And it won't be no hit and run. Full on war. To the death. Take no prisoners.

We was just about to climb out the cellar and make our way back to camp, when Ekt stopped me, and asked me again why I come back off patrol. He don't forget nothing, Ekt don't. So I told him we took a couple of prisoners, and he asked me who they was and where they come from. I don't know, I told him. Never seen them before. I don't think they come from the city. A couple of strangers passing through. Then he asked me can they fight, and I told him I thought one of them could, her looks tough, I said. What about the other one? he asked. No good, I said to him. Soft in the head by the looks on him. More like Kazz—

That warn't the right thing to say. I knowed it as I said it and tried to stop meself but it was too late. He stopped sudden and turned to me and I thought I was for it again. But he didn't do nothing. He just said, if he's like Kazz he ain't soft in the head.

And he walked on.

Lex was standing next to me and he grinned and slapped me on the shoulder. Have to be careful what we say about Kazz, he said. You know he won't hear nothing against her. And he said it all friendly-like, which is strange now I come to think about it, cos Lex ain't never been one for being friendly before. Not with me anyhow.

I ain't gonna give it too much thought, though. Only

one thing to think about now. And that's giving them
Geeks a thrashing. Gonna get me weapons and get me
blood up. Soon as we get back to camp. I can't wait.
Lex'll get we all together, and he'll give us the word and
we'll give it him back.

> *Ready for war?*
> *That's what we're for!*
> *To rumble and fight?*
> *We'll give it them right.*
> *Pound them and paste them!*
> *Wound them and waste them!*
> *Do them in, and do them good!*
> *Break their bones and drink their blood!*

Yeah.

Troggs: Ik

I ask her if she wants something to eat and she says no.

Ain't you hungry? I say.

No, she says.

I bet you are, I say.

You can bet what you like, she says.

What about him? I say.

Ask him, she says.

What's his name? I say.

Joey, she says.

What's yours? I say.

Mal, she says.

I'm Ik, I say. That's Kazz.

Great, she says. Now we all know each other we can be best friends.

I shrug. I'm only trying to be friendly. I never wanted to take them prisoner in the first place.

Is he your brother? I say.

No, she says. Why?

I don't know, I say. I just thought. Kazz is my sister.

He's not my brother, she says.

I call across to him, Hey, Joey, but he don't answer. I speak to him again.

Joey, I say. You want something to eat?

He don't even look round. He just stares straight ahead, into the dark. Like he ain't even heard me. Like he ain't hearing nor seeing nothing at all.

Joey

where it will happen   this is the place   here   this is
where it will happen   this is the place where it will
happen   here this place   this place here   it will happen here   here this is where   here is the place   where
it will happen   here   this is the place this is the place
here it will happen here   this is the place where it will
happen this is the place

Troggs: Ik

I ask her where they come from. We're both eating now, cold beans out of a can.

Another city, she says.

You're strangers here, then, I say.

That's right, she says.

Why did you leave your city, I ask her.

Because it's not there any more, she says.

It was the war, she tells me. Only a few managed to get out. Her and Joey were two of them. It happened about a year ago. They've been on the road since then.

Why'd you come here? I ask her.

This is where the road stopped, she says.

I ask her how they got in and she just says they found a way. Then she asks me why we took them. I tell her. I don't tell her I was against it, though.

This is our territory, I say.

Your territory? she say. What do you mean?

So then I tell her all about us and about the Geeks and how we've got our territory and they've got theirs, and we've got our goods and they've got theirs, and sometimes we raid each other, and steal each other's goods, and sometimes it comes to an all-out fight.

Why? she says.

We're at war, I say.

Why? she says.

Because we are, I say.

She shakes her head.

No escaping it, is there? she says. War out there, and war in here.

It's everywhere, I say. How it's always been, how it always will be.

No.

It's Kazz. I didn't think she'd been listening.

Not always, she says. And not for always. There was a time before. There'll be a time after.

She says things like that. Like it ain't her voice talking. Like it's something else. It's why Ekt thinks she's special. He says she can see things. I don't know what. It's ever since what happened to her. She wasn't like it before that. I wonder if I'd be like it if I'd have been there? Probably not. I'd have probably been killed along with the others.

Kazz nods towards Joey.

Ask him, she says. He knows.

Kazz

He sees what I see only I see it in shadow and he sees it clear, beyond war, beyond killing, beyond living, beyond dying, where the light shines and the flame burns bright.

He hears the wind in the flames, the terrible roaring, he hears the voices that cry out, that sing in the flames and out of the flames, voices wrapped in robes of flame, singing shining burning.

He shows me the picture, he has wings, he is flying, rising, falling upwards into the sun, into the flames, it is his dream, he is returning, becoming the flames, the light, becoming the bright burning.

From fire we come to fire we shall go from fire comes the shining

These are his words, only I hear them, words of light, words of flame, speaking out of the flame, he stands among them, he stands in flame, his voice speaking from the bright flame burning.

From the fire we come

From the fire he came, shining, burning.

Troggs: Ik

I can hear the others coming back. Hear them before I
see them. Saying the words.

Do them in, and do them good.

I know what that means.

The others are coming, I tell her.

I know, she says. I can hear them.

Looks like there's going to be a fight, I say.

How do you know? she says.

Listen, I say.

She listens. She nods.

Looks like there is, she says. Then she says, What's
going to happen to us? Me and Joey?

I shrug.

I don't know, I say.

She looks scared. I feel sorry for her. It was stupid
to take them. Pointless. Just Nasty being tough. And
nasty. Not thinking. He never thinks. He doesn't know
how to.

They won't bother with you much, I say. Not with a
fight coming. Maybe they'll just let you go.

I just said that. I know they won't.

She's looking round. Her eyes are working. Looking for a way out. She's thinking should she try and make a break for it. I'd have to stop her if she did, now the others are coming. If she'd tried before I'd have let her go. But it's too late now. She thinks it's too late as well. She stops looking round.

Had enough to eat? I ask her.

Yes, she says. Thanks. She's more friendly now. It's because we've been talking. Talking always makes you more friendly. I take the can and put it down. The others are nearer, their voices louder. Wilder. Pretty soon they'll be here. I can hear Nasty's voice above the others. He'll give himself a sore throat.

Joey, she says. Joey.

Joey doesn't answer her. Joey doesn't hear her.

Joey, she says again.

He's got something in his hands. I haven't seen it before.

What's he got there? I say.

Nothing much, she says. Just an old doll he found.

I go nearer and take a look. It's just what she said, a battered old doll. No hair. Looks like it's been in a fire. It's got feathers tied to its arms, black feathers. He holds it out to Kazz.

It's for you, he says to her.

She takes it. She holds it flat across her hands, looking down at it.

Hey, Kazz, I say to her. You're a bit old to be playing with dolls. She looks up at me.

It's not a doll, she says.
What is it, then? I say.
The Angel of Death, she says.
And she holds it up so that I can see it.

Mal

The others have come back. They're going to have a fight, and they're making me fight with them.

One of them has started a fire on a piece of waste-ground next to a building, some kind of old factory with no roof. They're standing round the fire clapping their hands and chanting, the same words they were chanting when they came back, over and over again. Each time a little louder, a little wilder. I can see their faces in the firelight, twisted by the flames, with open eyes and staring mouths. Not like human faces at all. Like masks they've put on. Their shadows flicker and curl across the wall of the old factory.

Ik sees me looking at them. He's helping me choose a weapon from a small pile of scrap metal.

'They always do that before a fight,' he says. 'Work themselves up. Lex is the one that gets them going. He reckons it makes them fight better.'

'Who's Lex?' I ask him. 'Is he the leader?'

Ik shakes his head.

'Ekt's Boss,' he says. 'Lex is second-in-command.'

I look across at them again. One of them jumps over

the fire, howling. The others cheer. Then another jumps, and another. I turn back to Ik.

'Why don't you join in?' I ask him.

'Sometimes I do,' he says. 'But it never takes hold of me like it takes them. Anyway, I'd rather have my head clear when I go into a fight.'

He holds out a flat piece of metal, about two feet long, rusty, with a spike at one end. It looks like broken railing.

'What's that?' I ask him.

'Yours,' he says. 'Your weapon. It'll do.'

I take it from him, weigh it in my hand. It's heavy, cold. You could crack somebody's skull open with it. Break their face. Put out their eyes. Maybe I should go across and join the others. Scream. Howl. Jump over the flames. I might as well. It's too late for anything else now. Too late for trying to get away. We're right in the middle of it, stuck here, me and Joey both, and there's no way out.

It happened like this.

When we heard them coming back I knew if we were going to get away it had to be then. Although Ik didn't say anything, I knew he wouldn't try to stop us. And his sister, Kazz, I could tell she wouldn't be any trouble. So I looked across at Joey, where he was sitting in front of the broken wall with the girl, trying to catch his eye, give him a signal. He understands things like that. Sometimes it's like he knows just what it is you're thinking. And I was thinking about making a break for it, thinking about it really hard. But he just wouldn't look at me. His eyes were fixed on the doll in his hands, staring at it like he couldn't see anything else. And the girl was staring at him. And there was a look on her face like she was frightened and excited at the same time.

Come on, Joey, I thought. Forget that doll for a minute. Look up. Look at me. Come on. We haven't got long. We've got to get away from here.

And then he spoke.

No. We must stay. This is where he has been leading us. Before us, bringing us to this place. Here.

All the time he was staring down at the doll. He didn't look at me, didn't move. But he spoke. I heard him. His voice inside my head, like a flame, burning. I felt stunned, lost, as if that flame that was his voice was growing brighter, fiercer, rising all around me, swallowing me up. And then it was gone. I was sitting there against the wall and Ik was asking me if I'd had enough to eat. No time had passed. But everything had changed. I was empty. My head was empty. Joey's words echoed inside it.

This is where it will happen, and we must stay until it's finished.

Where what will happen? I don't know the answer to that. I don't even think Joey does. All I know is I've got to go and be a part of this fight they're having, so I don't even know if I'll be coming back. I'm only glad that Joey hasn't got to go.

What happened was, as soon as the rest of the gang came back, one of them came over to us and said to Ik, 'We're having a fight.'

'I reckoned as much,' said Ik.

'Get our goods back,' she said. 'And this time we're going to smash them. Good and proper.'

'About time,' said Ik.

The girl grinned. 'Yeah,' she said. 'About time.' Then she looked at me. 'You've got to fight, and all.'

'Her?' said Ik. 'What for? She's just a trespasser—'

'Don't matter,' said the girl. 'She's here and she fights.' Then she nodded towards Joey. 'Not that other one, though. Nasty told us about him. Said he was some kind of loony. Like your sister.'

She grinned again. She's got a really horrible grin.

'You watch what you're saying about my sister, Ell,' said Ik. 'If Ekt was to hear you—'

'He can't hear me,' she said. 'And you ain't Ekt.' She looked at me again. 'We won't have no trouble off you, will we?' she said.

'Depends what kind of trouble you're after,' I said.

She stopped grinning, then, and stared at me, hard. She had a wrench in her hands and I thought she might take a swing at me with it. Then she laughed.

'Whatever trouble you got,' she said, 'just give it to the Geeks. They got all kinds of trouble coming at them.'

She turned back to Ik. 'Get her a weapon. We'll be going soon.'

She went back to the others and they started to make the fire.

I asked Ik what the fight was all about. If I was going to be part of it, I wanted to know why. He said what the girl had said, about getting their goods back. Then he told me what their goods were. Scrap. The pile of scrap metal I'm standing by now. This other gang stole some of their scrap. Now they're going to get it back. So that's why I'm standing here now with this piece of broken railing in my hands. Hearing them whooping, watching them jump over the flames, working themselves up for a fight over a pile of scrap metal. And it's stupid, it's got nothing to do with me, but I'm part of it, now, and there's no getting out of it.

Someone touches me on the arm. It's Ik.

'You'll be OK,' he says.

'How do you know?' I ask him.

He shrugs. 'I don't,' he says. 'But it's what I always tell myself. You'll be OK. And I have been so far.'

'There's always a first time,' I say to him.

'Yes,' he says, and he looks down, and I suddenly realize he's more scared than I am.

'Hey,' I say to him, and he looks up. 'You'll be all right.'

He grins. 'Yeah,' he says. 'We both will.'

The noise from the wasteground has stopped. The fire's still burning but everything's gone quiet. Then I see a figure walk out of the shadows by the old factory wall into the light of the fire. I hadn't noticed him before. He says something to the others, then turns and starts walking towards us. The others stay where they are, waiting.

Ik whispers to me. 'It's Ekt,' he says. 'The Boss.'

Like the others his clothes aren't much more than rags, but there's a way he has of wearing them that makes him seem different. With the others—and with me and Joey as well—they're just things we've grabbed and put on, stuff we've found or stolen and they don't fit us but it doesn't matter. But with Ekt what he's wearing seems right. It's the same filthy and tatty rags we all wear, but on him it looks like it belongs.

I take all this in as he's making his way towards us. When he gets to where we are he stops, and just looks at me for a while, like he's trying to work out who I am and where I've come from without having to go to the trouble of asking. Then he turns to Ik.

'What we got here, then, Ik?' His voice is soft. I hadn't expected that. 'A couple of trespassers?'

'Strangers,' says Ik. 'Just passing through. They didn't know it was our territory. I never wanted to take them. It was Nasty—'

'They're here now,' says Ekt. 'And they got to pay their way.'

'You could let them go,' says Ik.

Ekt shakes his head.

'Too late for that,' he says. 'We need them, now we got this fight with the Geeks. This one, anyway.' He looks at me. 'See you got yourself a weapon. I hope you can use it.'

'You'll soon find out,' I say. It's meant to sound tough, but I'm not sure it does.

Ekt grins.

'That's right,' he says. 'We will. What's your name?'

I tell him, and he nods, then he looks across at Joey. Joey's still sitting with his back against the wall. The girl Kazz is sitting next to him, with Joey's doll in her hands. She's staring at it.

'What about him?' he says to me.

'He's Joey,' I say.

'Nasty reckons he's a dummy,' says Ekt.

'He's not,' I say. 'He's just different.'

He turned to Ik.

'He said he was like Kazz,' he says.

'Nasty's stupid,' says Ik.

'He ain't clever,' says Ekt. 'Good fighter, though.'

Then Kazz looks up.

'He has my gift,' she says.

Ekt turns back to her.

'He sees things?' he says.

'It's in him strong,' she says. 'Stronger than in me. He was brought here.'

Ekt nods towards me. 'She brought him?' he says.

'No,' she says. 'Something else.'

Then she stands. Her hair's hanging down in knots and tangles around her face, but I can see her eyes burning through it. Suddenly everything seems to go very still, and I'm getting a tight feeling in my stomach. Her voice when she speaks again is a whisper, but it roars loud.

'He came out of the fire.'

There's a kind of flash inside my head and for a minute I'm not there any more. I'm standing in the square and the flames are rising and Joey's walking out and the flames are around him and he's holding something towards me. Then it's gone and I'm back and Kazz is holding the doll towards Ekt.

'What's that?' says Ekt.

'For luck,' she says. 'He made it. It has feathers. It flies. So you'll fly today.'

'You gonna sprout a couple of wings, then, Ekt?'

It's somebody else who's spoken, a voice I haven't heard before. I look round and see him, standing just behind Ik.

'That'll scare the shit out of the Geeks,' he says, 'seeing you come swooping down on them.'

He's not very tall, but his shoulders and arms are thick and heavy. His legs are the same, but somehow they seem too short for the rest of his body. He grins all the time he's talking, like everything he says, and every-thing everybody else says, he finds funny.

'She don't mean that, Lex,' says Ekt. 'She means we'll beat the Geeks.'

So this is Lex, the second-in-command. The one that was leading all that chanting and fire-jumping.

'Just you and that doll,' he says. 'That's all right, then. I'll go and tell the others they can stay here and leave you to it.'

He's got this long steel chain, part of it wrapped around his fist, the rest of it hanging down to the ground, and he keeps shaking it and twisting it round and round so that it clinks and rattles. I stare at it, the way it catches the moonlight, cold and hard.

'They'll be disappointed though,' he says. 'I've got them all worked up now and they're ready for it. Ready for anything. You ready, Ik?'

Ik starts to say something but he doesn't wait to hear it and speaks to me.

'What about you?' he says. 'You ready for anything?'

I look up from the chain. My head's still full of what the girl, Kazz, said about Joey, him being brought here and coming out of the flames, and how she could have known about all that. And it's full as well of everything that's happened since we came here and suddenly none of it seems real. It's like everything's behind glass and I'm on one side of the glass looking through and everything else is on the other side, even Joey. So when I speak, my voice sounds really loud, like I'm trying to make myself heard through that glass.

'Ready for anything,' I say. 'Just give the word.'

And it's not even my voice speaking. It's somebody else, coming from a long way off.

'There you go,' says Lex to Ekt. 'Everybody's ready.'

'Better go and do it, then,' says Ekt.

The girl Kazz is still standing there with the doll with the crow's feathers tied to it holding it out to Ekt.

'Will you take it?' she says to him.

He looks at the doll, and glances at Lex. Lex just stands there grinning, the chain hanging from his fist, rattling. Then he looks back at Kazz.

'Yeah,' he says, and takes it from her. He stuffs it inside his jacket.

'Let's go,' he says, and moves off, and Lex follows him.

All this time Joey hasn't moved or looked up or said anything. He's still sitting there with his back against the broken wall.

'Joey?' I say to him, and now he raises his head and looks at me.

'It will be all right,' he says. And then, 'It's meant.'

I speak to the girl.

'Look after him,' I say to her, then Ik touches me on the shoulder.

'We'd better go.'

The moon's low in the sky and though it's still dark there's that early-morning feel, just before the grey light comes. I grip the piece of railing tight in my fist and we walk past the junk and across the open space towards where the fire still burns and the others are waiting.

Geeks: Schyte

Well I'm still on lookout ain't I been here all night and
not even Fig an' her stinky old coat to keep me company,
only once somebody come up to bring me something and
that was Jax and all he brought me was half a tin a cold
soup and half a tater and it tasted like a rat or something
had died in it. Well I ate it cos I was hungry and I asked
him if they'd had their council of war yet and he said,
Yes, and they was all armed and ready and just waiting
for Ekt and the rest of the Troggs to turn up, and that
might be anytime now, he said. So then he said, No
slacking, Schyte, and keep your eyes sharp cos we'll be
wanting to know the minute they're here. And I said to
him, You saying I'm a slacker, and he said, I ain't saying
nothing, I'm just saying keep your eyes sharp. Well I let
it go at that. I wasn't going to give him no grief nor get
none from him neither. He's a big bugger is Jax, what
he ain't got in brains he makes up for in muscle and
he ain't somebody you want to get on the wrong side of
him if you can help it.

He left just after that and I finished the soup and
the half a tater and that was about an hour ago or

something like that and it's like I ain't ate nothing at all and I'm wishing I could sneak off like I do sometimes and go down to the canal and find that old bloke who keeps that store of food and trade a tin of something off him. Only I can't can I cos if I was to go you can bet that'd be when the Troggs showed up and if I don't give the warning I'll be for it. So here I am hungry and cold and still looking out the window at them same old empty streets and broke down buildings. It ain't so deep dark now, kind of a smoky grey and the moon's gone. Still freezing though I can see me breath all icy and me hands am hurting even when I shove them through me jumper under me armpits.

If they'm coming they'll be coming soon and I wish they'd hurry up cos I hate just standing around and waiting. It's the waiting that's the worst of it when there's going to be a fight. Once it starts and you get stuck in it's all right then, you don't have to think about anything, just let the fighting take over and do the work for you. A raid's better, there ain't no waiting around like this when you'm on a raid, you got the planning and the sneaking up and taking your positions, then Akh gives the word and in you go yelling and screaming to put the frights into them, and then it's crash bang thump and out and off again before they know what's hit them. That's how it was last time we had a run-in with the Troggs, the time we got all their goods, and it was great, I give that Uba a real kicking, he didn't even see me coming. That's what they'm so sore about, us taking them like that and getting their goods, and it's why they'm coming now to have it out with us and try get their goods back. And if they do we'll just have to go and get them again, and if they don't they'll come back and try again. That's how it's been since the beginning, and that's how it'll go on, I suppose, till it's settled between us one way or another once and for all.

Still no sign of them out there, nothing moving. There ain't never nothing moving out there, ain't nobody except us lives down this end no more. All the people that lived in them houses and walked in them streets am dead or gone off. Them what was left alive moved away to the centre, and who remembers them now, who they was and what they did? Blowed away by the war, like the people in the old hospital where we got our headquarters. All them was blowed away and all. Akh says as how a shell dropped straight on top of it and the whole thing went up in flames and smoke. He was here, he says, he seen it, and he reckons how sometimes he can still see it, the fire burning and hear them what was inside screaming. He reckons how everything that happens in a place it's still happening all the time if you can just kind of tune yourself into it, not just bad things like the hospital burning but ordinary things too, people living their lives in a place, what they did and what happened to them, it's all still there, you just got to tune into it, he says. I don't like it when he talks like that, it gives me the creeps, but you can't say nothing, can you, cos he's Boss. Sometimes I think he says it just to wind we up and sometimes I think it's all true and he's got himself tuned right into it, cos there's something scary about him, a kind of light in his eyes and that's why he don't never get hurt when we have a fight, he don't get so much as a scratch while the rest of we get beat up somehow or other, even Jax. Ain't nothing can touch him, Jax said to me once, and I reckon he's right.

Thinking about them things that Akh says and looking out at the old broke streets and houses gets me all wired tight and I'm thinking maybe I'm getting tuned in or something and in a minute I'll start seeing things, and just as I think that there's a shadow moves in a doorway just across the street. Well me guts just turn over don't they and I make a smell so bad it makes me eyes water, then that shadow comes out of the doorway and there's other follow it onto the street, and it's what I should've knowed straight off, ain't it, it's the Troggs come for the fight.

There's Ekt in front with Lex, and Yass, Nasty and Ell and Uba and Ik, and there's another one I ain't never seen before, a girl her is, walking next to Ik. Her's only small, thin and scraggy-looking, and her don't look very old neither, so I think to meself I'll make for her when the fight starts up cos with all that and being a new recruit and all, her'll be easy target. I ain't that big meself, and I'd rather tangle with somebody like her rather than the likes of Nasty or Ell. And I'm thinking all this while

I'm sneaking out the back of the house, running down the alley, over the wall, and onto the wasteground full of bricks from blowed-up houses, and across the other side which is where our headquarters am, and in front of that is the barricade we built one end of the wasteground to the other to stop the Troggs making a sneak attack on we like we made on them, and standing in front of that with their weapons is Akh and the rest of them.

So I run up to them and I say, They'm coming, and Rok says Good, and Jax says, Let's have them, and Little Jax says, Yeah, right, let's have them, cos he can't say nothing but what Jax says. And good and proper this time, Dis puts in, and Fig just grins and smacks her weapon in the flat of her hand, and you can tell they'm ready for it, they got that look, and I got that look meself, I can feel it on me face, that grin like what Fig's got. You OK now, I ask her, Yeah, she says, no thanks to you. I let that go cos we got other things to think about now, and then I remember and I tell them about the new recruit they got, A girl I ain't seen before, I say. The more the better, says Rok, we can show her what it's about, then Akh he speaks for the first time, and all he says is, Ready then? and we all say Yeah. Right then, he says, let's go, and the sky's starting to get light up there above the buildings, pale and cold-looking with little streaks of red, and we'm feeling good and we set off across the wasteground to meet them and give them what for.

 Kazz

We sit together by the wall, our backs resting against it, the two of us alone now because the others have gone, but of course not alone really, the dead are always with us.

The canal is there with ice on the water, broken in places, and the light coming now, broken like the ice, and across the canal the streets and houses and factories broken too, and broken the city that was once a place of wonder.

I start to tell him about the city, that all was not now as it is, there were tall buildings that rose to the sun, and wide streets and fountains, a city of marvels, it was, and a great tree I remember, a tree of shining metal, and its leaves—

Its leaves fluttered and sang like birds.

His voice speaks the words before I speak them, he sees what I see, my memory, but how did he see it, is it his memory too, were you here ever, or was there such a tree in your city, I ask him.

I don't come from any city.

I say to him, where from then, and he says nothing,

but again I see the flames and him among them, only now there's something else, there are wings in the flames, great wings spread above him, and he is not harmed, and then what he shows me is gone.

I take his hand, it's cold, I press it to bring warmth, place it against my face, my eyes closed feeling his hand on my face, and I say to him, with you it is the fire, with me it is the mist, a mist and figures moving through it, they whisper to me the words I must speak, but if truth or tale I can't tell, nor if it's gift or curse.

It's both.

Yes, yes, gift and curse, the dead who speak through me, and they were not always here, they came with the war, and I show him and he sees, fire from the sky and a thunder, and the house we lived in tumbled about us, all dead, and I lay buried with them, I thought I was of them, but they began to whisper, no, there is something you must do, one yet to be saved, and after that you will return, but we will make a gift, which is the language of the dead, which you will speak, for we see what the living cannot, so I found him who was to be saved, and we came back into the light, though there is always the mist where the dead walk and whisper, and it's their language I speak, though none listen, only he who was saved.

And now me.

And now you, but there is another language you speak, it is the language of fire, and what comes out of

76

the fire, it speaks and you listen, you follow where it leads, then he shows me something else, there are high mountains, the sun and the moon in the mountains, days of heat, nights of cold, he walks among them, and the girl with him, but there is another who walks ahead, sometimes in flame, sometimes in mist in shadow, a winged creature, terrible and fierce, a creature to be feared, it leads them through the mountains, and down from the mountains, and there ahead is a wide plain, the walls of a city, an old man of rags and bones, a bird in a cage, then the cage is open, the bird flies to the sun, its feathers are fire, and they enter the city, but the guide is gone.

This is what he shows me, the story of his coming here, his hand still against my face, my hand laid upon it, and now he turns his hand and takes mine, pressing it, his hand holding my hand, and I say to him, it was meant your coming here, I see that, but not the reason for it, and he is going to speak and give answer, but suddenly there is something else in his eyes, a new picture, I do not see it, then the words come, fast and hard, speaking through him.

He gives a shout and they all shout and then you're running—

His hand squeezing mine, hurting, and the words coming, then the picture, I begin to see it, and the noise, the voices shouting, screaming, and the words coming.

—and the others are shouting too and running too and your head's on fire and your blood's pumping—

He can see it, the fight, he's with them—
—then you're in with a kick and somebody's down—
—and I see it too, and am with them too—
—and you make them stay down and you keep on kicking—
—there among them, the fists, the faces—
—swing the metal, smash the face—
—all's heat, all's fire, and a hand grabs my hair—
—he gets you in the ribs and you're down on your knees—
—and he's there above me, ready to strike—
—hammer your skull, spill your brains—
—but there's a knife in my hands—
—you slam upwards—
—thrust in deep—
—twist, turn—
—and I feel his weight, and there's blood on my hands—
—and you're up on your feet and there's nobody left—
—they're running, it's over—
—over, it's over.
It's over, his hand looses mine, he breathes deep and slow, and the picture is gone, but this was more than picture, more than showing and seeing, this was living it, being here and being there at the same time, and it's for this he has come, and it's terrible for him, not only to see but to live such things, a suffering, worse than fire or flame, look I say to him, look, it's light now, the sun's

in the sky, the dark's gone, we're here, it's all right, saying these things over and over, it's all right, taking his hand again, it's all right, stroking his face, the day's here, it's all right now, it's over, and his words whisper like the words of the dead.

It's never over.

Troggs

'We beat them!'
  'They run!'
  'Scarpered, scattered!'
  'Got our goods back!'
  'Got their goods, and all!'
  'Wasted them!'
  'Shafted them!'
  'Mangled and maimed them—'
  'Gutted and brained them!'
  'Did them in!'
  'Did them good!'
  'Broke their bones and drank their blood!'
  'You fought well.'
  'Do you think so?'
  'Like you was one of us.'
  'Did you see how they run? Did you see it?'
  'I was there! I seen it!'
  'Like the devil was after them!'
  'I had one down. "Don't hit me!" he said.'
  'What did you do?'
  'I hit him, smack in the teeth!'

'They know who's top gang, now.'
'Yeah, they know that, all right.'
'And it's all down to Ekt.'
'Ekt, the Boss!'
'Boss of the whole place!'
'Boss of everywhere!'
'Boss of the world!'
'Ekt! YEAH!'
'That doll brought we luck after all.'
'Let's see it! Show us the doll!'
'Here it is!'
'It's got wings!'
'Crow feathers!'
'The doll, YEAH!'
'The crow-doll, YEAH!'
'YEAH!'
'YEAH!'
'And him what brought the doll!'
'Where is he?'
'Over here!'
'What's his name?'
'Joey, ain't it?'
'Yes, Joey.'
'Here he is!'
'He's the one!'
'He gave we the doll!'
'He brought we luck.'
'He helped we win!'

'Beat the Geeks!'
'Joey, YEAH!'
'Joey and his doll!'
'Joey and his crow-doll!'
'Joey the crow-boy!'
'Joey the crowboy!'
'The Crowboy!'
'The Crowboy!'
'Crowboy! YEAH!'

Joey

they dance me in the air   I'm up and above them and
they're below and they dance me nothing else above
only the sun and the sky   and they dance me in the
sun dance me in the sky   there's laughing   there are
voices   they dance me it's like flying   up in the air
and here is where it starts   this is the beginning   and
there's the sun and it's laughing and I'm laughing
and they're laughing   crowboy   crowboy   spread my
wings   I'm the crowboy come to save them   dancing
flying laughing   the beginning

Troggs: Ik

Yeah, we beat them.

Beat them like we said we would, good and proper.

Yeah, we sent them running, scarpering, scattered them, broke through their barricade.

Yeah, we got our goods back. Got their goods too. Now they haven't got anything, and we're top gang.

Yeah, we broke a few faces, cracked some ribs, smashed some teeth. And it felt good, at the time it felt good, like it always does, at the time.

But we killed one of them.

Rok, it was. I saw his body lying there, blood on his chest, blood on the ground. The blood was coming out of a hole in his chest.

The others was over the barricade, in their camp, wrecking it, getting our goods and theirs. The Geeks had run off. There was only me and him. Me standing on the wasteground and him lying there with the blood coming out of the hole in his chest.

I knew Rok. He was Akh's second. I've spoke to him. I could see it was Rok but it didn't look like him. His eyes was closed. But he didn't look like he was sleeping. He looked like he was dead.

Somebody had a knife. One of us. I don't know who. I didn't see who did it. But somebody had a knife and somebody killed him.

Nobody's saying, but everybody knows. They're laughing, larking about, got Joey up on their shoulders, carrying him around. Everybody's having a party, even her. But they know, like I know.

Somebody's dead.

That makes things different.

Everything's changed.

Nothing won't be the same again.

Geeks: Akh

We stand around his body. Nobody says anything. They're waiting for me to speak. I don't say anything. I look at them. Jax's face is swollen down one side. Fig has a big cut across the top of her head and her hair's matted with blood. Schyte's nose is broken. Little Jax can hardly walk and Dis is holding on to him. A right bunch. Any one could be lying where Rok's lying and I wouldn't miss them.

They're still waiting for me to speak. I still don't say anything. I kneel down beside him and touch his face. It's cold. About as cold as I feel. I stay down there, my hand on his face.

They start to talk.

'One of them had a knife,' says Schyte.

'Which one?' says Jax.

'I don't know,' says Schyte. 'I didn't see.'

'How do you know they had a knife, then?' says Fig.

'They must've done,' says Schyte.

'He's right,' says Dis, 'for once. Must've been a knife.'

'We always said no knives,' says Little Jax. 'That's what we always said. No knives.'

I listen to them, I hear all they say. But it's just words and don't mean anything.

'They di'n't play fair,' says Schyte. 'That's why they beat us, cos they di'n't play fair.'

'It was more than that,' says Dis.

'What do you mean?' says Jax.

'I ain't sure,' says Dis. 'There was something about them. Something different. The way they come at us. The way they come at us, like—' And he stops. Then he says, 'I don't know. There was just something about them.'

'I know what you mean,' says Schyte, 'something different, yeah. There was that girl, for a start, that new recruit. She was wild, she was, crazy.'

'Yeah,' says Fig. 'I seen you running away from her.'

'I wasn't the only one to run,' says Schyte, 'we all run, all of we run.'

'You showed we how to do it,' says Fig.

They start having a go. Then the others join in. I've had enough. It's time to put a stop to it.

'All right,' I say, and they shut up. I stand. 'Let's deal with Rok,' I say to them. 'We'll take him to the canal.'

They don't look easy with it. It's Little Jax who speaks up.

'That's their territory,' he says.

'I know,' I say. 'I don't care. Let them try and stop us.'

They lift him onto their shoulders, Jax, Dis, Fig, Schyte. I tell Little Jax to bring some bricks, four big ones. I go in front. Little Jax is at the back, carrying the bricks, limping. We make our way across the wasteground then down into the street. We go past the houses, then come to the place where the old factories are. Their territory. I can smell it. We take a left and go through a narrow gap between two buildings, then out across some rough ground, over a fallen-down wire fence, and down onto the gravel path that leads to the canal.

They put him down on the path. It's a bright morning. The air's biting cold. The canal's frozen over. I tell them to break it up. Jax and Dis find a couple of big wooden stakes and use them to smash the ice. I take the bricks off Little Jax and stuff them into Rok's clothes so they won't come out. The others stand back, and I kneel down and push his body off the towpath into the water. It rolls in and smashes through the ice and sinks through the black water into the sludge at the bottom. I stand up and stare at the water till it's settled again, flat and still and just the ice glittering in the light.

'Right,' I say to the others. 'Let's get back. We've got things to do.'

They start making their way back up the gravel path. I turn to follow them and look up along the canal. This stretch of it is dead straight, and right up towards the top I can see the lock where the Troggs have their camp. There's somebody standing on the lock-gate. Just standing there, looking down the canal. He's a long way off, but I can see his face clear and sharp, and it's not any-body I've seen before. We both stay like that for a minute or so, then he drops down off the lock-gate and he's gone.

It's cold. My hands are hurting with it, burning. I look up the gravel path where the others are walking towards the factories, making their way back to the camp. Rok was my best mate. We came through a lot together. I'd rather have him than any of the others put together.

They're going to pay for it.

Mal

It's almost evening, the light's starting to fade, and my left arm really hurts.

It's only just started to bother me. I've been pretty high all day, but that's gone now, and the pain's come, a deep throbbing inside my arm. I suppose it's been there all the time, but I didn't notice it. I was up there somewhere with all the others. Flying with Joey and his magic doll. I'm back with a thump now. Dropped from a great height. That's how it feels.

I push up my sleeve and take a look. The whole of my lower arm is bruised and swollen, and I can't move my fingers very well. It must have happened during the fight, I suppose, but I don't remember it. Whoever hit me must've put some weight behind it. It looks nasty. I don't think it's broken. I think it would look worse than this if it was broken.

It looks bad enough, though, and it really is starting to hurt now.

I reach down with my right hand into the canal and grab a lump of ice and press it against the bruise. The cold bites into the pain and takes it away so I keep the ice there until I can't stand the cold any more, and I drop it back into the water. After a while the cold goes and the throbbing pain starts up again.

They've lit another fire over on the wasteground. All the scrap metal we took is piled up there. They've been working at it all day and they still haven't finished. Once they've made it into a pile, they stand back, look at it, then take the pieces off and start again. Build it up, and take it down again, over and over. As if they're trying to make it perfect. As if there's a perfect way of piling it up.

Joey's over there with them. Maybe he's the one who makes them keep taking it down and piling it up again. It's the kind of thing he'd do. They'd do it for him as well. They'd do anything he told them, right now. He's their hero, their Crowboy. Helped them beat the Geeks, helped them get their goods. With his strange magic powers. So that's what we came here for. To help some gang steal a load of scrap.

Big deal.

There must be more to it than that. If not, there's just no sense to it, no sense to anything. And there has to be some kind of sense to things. The reason why they fight over this scrap, for one. There has to be a reason for it. I asked one of them about it, his name's Uba, I think, and he just shrugged and looked at me like nobody had ever asked that question before, like he'd never even thought about it, which he probably hadn't.

'I don't know,' he said. 'We just do. I mean, there ain't nothing else, is there? So it's got to be that.'

Crazy.

But I suppose no more crazy than anything else that people do. When the war came to our city people did crazy things there as well. Like when they killed all the dogs. It made sense at first. Food started to run out so they caught dogs and killed them to eat. After they'd skinned them and cut the meat off they threw the bones out in the streets. People started collecting the bones, first of all any bones, then just the skulls. Then they started knocking the teeth out of the skulls and making necklaces out of them. Soon everybody was wearing them. You weren't anybody unless you had at least one necklace of dog's teeth. Some people had two or three strung round their necks. I had one myself. I didn't make it, though. Somebody gave it to me. Strange, I can't remember who it was, now. Somebody I knew then. It was a long time ago.

The throbbing in my arm suddenly gets really bad, and I take another lump of ice out of the canal and hold it against the pain. The cold water runs through my fingers. The sun's starting to go down and above the buildings the sky's turning a deep red, but higher up the blue's fading to grey and there are a few stars. There's one star that's very bright, low down in the sky. I think about the night before, Joey standing on the edge of the canal, holding the doll up, pretending it was flying. The feathers he tied to the doll. What he said about the dead bird and the star being the same thing. Now he's over there trying to get that pile of scrap just right. It's like all the time he's trying to put things together, things that are broken, trying to make a pattern out of them. As if he knows that everything does fit into some kind of pattern, and that's what he has to do. Find the pattern and fit everything into it.

Maybe that's why he brought us here. Because we're part of that pattern.

'That looks bad.'

It's Ik. I didn't hear him come up.

'It is pretty bad,' I say to him.

'Let's have a look,' he says.

I take the ice away from my arm. He looks at it.

'Yeah,' he says. 'It's bad. Does the ice help?'

'A bit,' I say.

He doesn't say anything for a while, and just stares at my arm as if he's trying to think of something that will make it better. Then he just says, 'It's cold. You ought to go over to the fire.'

'I will in a bit,' I say.

He nods, then looks away across the canal, and asks me if I've seen Kazz and Ekt.

'No,' I say. 'I haven't seen them for a while. I don't know where they are.'

That seems to upset him, like he was counting on

me to know, but he only shrugs and says, 'They'll be around. I'll find them.'

He stands there for a while looking out across the canal, like he's wanting to talk about something, and I know what it is, and he's waiting for me to start. But I don't say anything. Over on the wasteground they seem to have finished building the scrap-pile. Maybe Joey's happy with it now. Somebody shouts and somebody laughs, and then they're all laughing. Then their laughter stops.

'Well,' says Ik, 'I hope your arm feels better soon.'

'I suppose it will,' I say. Then I say, 'Ik—' but he's already walking away, down to the lock-gate. He climbs onto the gate and walks across it and drops down onto the other side. Then he walks towards the old factories, and turns a corner, and he's gone.

I know what it was he wanted to talk about. He reckons we killed somebody.

We were all celebrating, just after we got back from the fight. They had Joey up on their shoulders and they were carrying him around, because they believed that somehow he'd given them some kind of power, and I believed it too then as well, and we were all shouting and whooping and laughing, and Joey was laughing too, laughing up there on their shoulders. Only Ik wasn't laughing. He wasn't joining in. He was standing apart, just staring at us. Then suddenly he shouted out:

'What about the one we killed!'

Everybody stopped. Nobody said anything. Ik said, 'We killed one of them.'

Then Ekt said, 'What are you talking about, Ik?'

'It was Rok,' said Ik. 'I saw him. Somebody stabbed him. He's dead.'

Ekt turned to us.

'Anybody know anything about this?'

There was silence again.

'Anybody else see it?' said Ekt. Then Lex spoke.

'Looks like it was just Ik,' he said. 'Maybe he's started seeing things. Like his sister.'

Somebody sniggered. I think it was Nasty. Ekt suddenly looked angry and he was about to say something, when Ik shouted, 'I wasn't seeing things! Somebody killed Rok! One of us killed him!'

'Stabbed him, you said,' said Lex. 'Like with a knife.'

'That's right,' said Ik. 'With a knife.'

'But we ain't got no knives,' said Lex. He looked at Ekt. 'That's right, ain't it, Ekt? Knives ain't allowed. That's our rule.'

'That's it,' said Ekt. 'Anybody had a knife, I'd know about it.'

'So he can't have been stabbed,' said Lex. 'So he can't be dead. So you must've been seeing things.'

There was a dazed look on Ik's face. He stared round at us all, like he was waiting for one of us to speak up for him, but nobody did. Then he looked straight at Ekt.

'Ekt. I saw him. Dead.'

Ekt shook his head. When he spoke, he wasn't looking at Ik.

'I ain't sure, Ik. You know what it's like. Things get mixed up. It's hard to know what you see and what you don't—'

Ik cut in and his voice was hard and flat.

'I know what I saw. And somebody else here does too.'

He turned and walked off. As he did, somebody made a farting sound, and we all laughed, and it was only after, when I came down out of it and my arm began to hurt, that I felt bad about it.

I feel bad about it still. I feel bad for Ik, but I don't know what to say to him, because I feel even worse for myself. I've started thinking about the fight, now, thinking about what happened and how it felt. And I've started to understand something about it too, and that's what it is that's getting to me.

I'm looking at the water in the canal. It's flat and still, and the ice is glittering in the evening light, flickering like little flames across the surface. But it's like I can see through the glittering, right down to the bottom. I can see what lies at the bottom. All the stuff people have thrown in there over the years, all the junk they wanted to get rid of, it's still down there, twisted and broken in the black sludge. It doesn't go away. And once you've seen it you can't forget it's there.

I look away from the water, back towards the wasteground. I can see Joey coming across the wasteground towards me. He's carrying some scrap in his arms. And a little way off there's Lex, standing on his own. He's watching Joey as Joey walks towards me. Just standing there watching. For some reason it makes me feel uneasy. But I'm glad Joey's coming. I roll my sleeve back over my arm and look back at the water. A few minutes later I hear Joey come up. There's a clatter as he drops the scrap he was carrying onto the ground. Then he sits down in front of it.

'What you doing with that?' I ask him.

He's staring at the scrap.

'There's a picture,' he says.

'In your head,' I say.

He nods. 'I have to make it.'

'A picture of what,' I ask him. 'What are you going to make?'

He doesn't say anything for a while. Then he says, 'It's like the doll.' He grins. 'Only bigger.'

'It's a good job you made that doll,' I say to him. 'It saved our skins, I reckon. They think it was your doll helped them win. I don't know, maybe they're right, maybe it did.'

I'm working up to telling him, now, the thing I've been waiting to tell him, I can feel it getting ready to come out.

'Only trouble is,' I say, 'it means we're stuck here. For a while, anyway. They won't want you to go. You're their lucky mascot.'

'Crowboy,' he says.

'That's right. The Crowboy. And they won't want their Crowboy to go running off.' It's ready, now, I'm going to tell it. 'Nor me. I'm a good fighter. That's what they said. A good fighter. And you know what, Joey? I am. I am a good fighter. Listen. Let me tell you about it. Let me tell you what it was like.'

Then I try to tell him.

Joey

she is speaking but she is not speaking she is sitting by
the water and the water is on fire and there are no
words *first off I was scared* there are no words to say
it and she tries to find them and she can't *and my
blood was rushing* because there are no words but
the water is on fire the ice burning tongues of flame
and the flame speaks *and this blood-red light burning*
out of the burning come the words I hear the words
I hear the flame speaking *it made me feel alive* it tells
me what she can't because there are no words but there
are words in the flame that burns on the water *there
was blood on my hands* and I hear them

Mal

first off I was scared, never been so scared
I felt sick, I thought I was going to be sick
then we were running, there were faces and shouting
and it started, and my fear went,
and my blood was rushing, my heart banging
this blood-red light burning in my head
I didn't know what I was doing
but I kept on doing it
something in me took over
something I never knew was there
something that howled and raged and roared
something that danced on an altar of bones
and it made me feel alive
my whole body awake and alive
nerves singing, skin on fire
as if I was alive for the first time
as if I'd never been alive before
and then it was over
and when it was over
my arms ached, my throat was raw
there were cuts on my face

there was blood on my hands
I was shaking and I didn't want it to be over
and now I know something
something I didn't know before
I know something about the war
why it happened, why it keeps on happening
it happens because we want it to
because it makes us feel alive
the thing that howls and rages and roars
the thing that dances on the altar of bones
it lives in us, it lives through us
it's what we are when we're truly alive
and that's why it happens, why it keeps on happening
that's why it happens, because we want it

Mal

I shake my head, blink, look round, and I'm back.

Still here by the canal. Joey still here. The scrap he brought over. My arm still hurting. But it's darker. Colder. The light gone from the water. And it's all changed. As if everything's been taken and turned inside out, and now it's turned back again, and it looks the same but it's not the same at all.

And where was I when that happened? I was back there in the fight, living it again. And Joey was there, living it with me. Now he knows without my telling him. He knows deeper than if I had been able to tell him. I couldn't find the words. He found them for me.

I look out across the canal, to the old factories, and beyond the old factories, the sky, darkening fast now, the stars brighter. And there's an emptiness. And it seems that everything I look at is looking into me, and there's an emptiness there as well. Then the emptiness fills up suddenly and spills over and there are tears on my face and my throat aches and it hurts and it won't stop.

'What are we going to do, Joey?' I say to him. 'Why have we come here? What's going to happen to us?'

At first I don't think he's heard me. He just sits, staring at that little pile of scrap. Then he lifts his hand, touches my hair, strokes it. One finger brushes the skin at the side of my face. In all the time we've been together, he's never touched me. When he speaks his voice is soft.

'It's all right,' he says. 'You'll be all right.'

Then he says, 'Tomorrow I'll build it.'

I don't ask him what he means. I know I'll find out. I turn my head and look across at the wasteground again. It's almost dark. The fire's burning, bright and fierce. I can see the others sitting around it. They're not making any sound. And Lex is gone.

Troggs: Lex

He's got to go. Crowboy, Crazyboy, whatever they've called him. Her too, the girl. I watched her fight. She's good, too good. That's the last thing I want. I had it all worked out, and it was going fine. Ell and Uba were with me. And I'd started work on Nasty. He wouldn't have taken long. Just told him we'd be getting rid of Ik and Kazz and he'd have been there, no problem. Yass would've been a bit trickier, but he's for the gang and anything that's good for the gang. He'd have come round, yeah. All it was gonna take was for us to get beat one more time. Then I'd have made my move. Easy, no problem. What's that sound?

Nothing. A rat. Coming out of the building there. Crossing the alley. Where's it going? Sniffing, looking for something. What you looking for? Something to eat. They'll eat anything. Saw one eating another rat once. A live rat eating a dead rat. Could've been one of its brothers, its mother. It didn't care. Needed to eat and it ate. That's how they are. That's how it is. What you looking at? Yeah, it's you I'm talking about.

Then they come along. Straight off I had a bad feeling.

Something about him. I knew he was bad news. Going in to the fight I knew. We're gonna win, we're gonna beat them. Shit. I had to think on my feet. Think fast. Couldn't let that be the end of it. Had to give Akh a real good reason to come back after us. Good thing I had the knife. Good thing nobody knows about it.

Still sharp. Need to keep it sharp. On this stone. A good edge. Bright. I like the sound it makes. That rat's gone.

It ain't enough, though. We've got to lose. When they come after us. Lose bad. That's the whole point. But we can't lose, now, can we? Not now we got our lucky mascot. Good old Crowboy. Crap. There ain't nothing lucky about him. He's just a dummy, like Kazz is a dummy. Kids sent crazy by the war. The trouble is, though, the rest of them believe it. And that's what counts. Believing it. They feel lucky. Feel like Top Gang and they can't be beat. They're Top Gang and Ekt's Top Boss. So where does that leave me? Out in the shithouse with my trousers round my feet.

Test the edge. On my thumb. No pressure. Nice and gentle. Straight through. Easy as that. Didn't feel a thing. You don't let yourself. Now the blood. Dark, running down my hand. Warm. The taste of it. That sharp taste.

I need to get things back like they were. Need the Geeks to come after us and for us to get beat. I mean really beat, good and thrashed. Point the finger at Ekt.

Put the blame on him. Then I can step in. Take his place. Just like I should've done at the start. And there's only one way that's going to happen.

They've got to go. What's that? Another rat?

Look who it is. Ekt. With her. As usual. Been off somewhere together. Listening to her tell his fortune. Good job she's just a crazy. If she could tell it he wouldn't like what he heard. Maybe she'll have to go as well. And that brother of hers. And one or two more.

Here they come. Put the knife away. Stand up. Walk towards them. Raise my hand. Smile.

How's it going, brother?

Part Two

Orf

So I'm back in the city after me usual rounds, making me way along the towpath to me den, only this time me rounds ain't been so usual, and I ain't feeling none too easy. I'm earlier than usual, as well, it's still only afternoon, and though the sun's on its way down it's bright and clear and the light's coming sharp off the ice on the canal. The air's sharp and all, slicing through me chest and I'm a bit short of breath. As a rule I ain't back till it's getting dark or after, and I ain't walking so light as this neither, and that's on account of I ain't brought back nothing from out there today, except what I seen, and that's what it is why I ain't feeling easy.

The thing is, there ain't near so much in the way of pickings and takings as there used to be, hardly nothing at all worth going out for, never mind bringing back. So today I decided to scout round a bit further out, down alongside the river. I reckoned it'd be safe enough, seeing as the troops are all camped on the other side, and they only come across when there's a fight to be had, and, like I said, there ain't been one of them for a while now. Except for that bit of a skirmish the other day, when I got me last good haul. And that didn't look like it was what you might call real fight.

Now there's one part where you can see clear across the plain to the river, but further on there's a place where the ground rises up to a ridge with a few trees and bushes growing on top. Through the trees and out the other side and the ridge drops down sharp again to the river, and it was there I was going to have a look. There was fighting over there in the early days, like there was everywhere, and I'd made meself more than a few good hauls. Course, I'd pretty much picked the place clean since them days, but the place is such a tangle there might be something I'd missed. That's what I was thinking anyway as I was climbing up the ridge. The other thing I was thinking was that there was less chance of me being spotted by the troops on the other side while I was going about me business, owing to that same tangle of trees and bushes.

But no sooner had I got meself up the top than I heard noises coming from down by the river, so I dropped low and crawled forward and took a gander to see what was going on. There was soldiers everywhere, all along the riverbank. They'd built some kind of a makeshift bridge and was moving stuff across from one side to the other—lots of boxes mostly that each one took two of them to carry. I guessed straight off what was in them boxes and why it was they was bringing them across just here where they couldn't be seen, and

I knew as well I wasn't going to get no pickings there, so I slid meself back through the trees and down the ridge and come back to the city.

So that's why I ain't feeling none too easy. It's certain they're getting ready for a surprise attack and by the looks of things it won't be too long in coming. They won't hit so bad down here where I am, of course. It's pretty deserted, and has been for ages, except for the gangs. And I reckon I'll be keeping away from the centre. That's where all hell's going to be let loose when it starts. So I'll just keep me head down till it's done, then pack up what I can and move on. Well nothing lasts, does it? It's the way things are, and there's plenty more cities like this. Funny thing is, though, thinking about what's coming brings to mind them two kids I come across a few days back, them as I showed the way in. And especially him, the lad, and that trick he pulled with the dead crow. If they'd known then what was coming they wouldn't have been so keen to get inside. It looked to me when I seen them they'd had theirselves a good plateful of trouble already without shovelling more on. Then again, who knows? Maybe they just couldn't get enough of it. Come looking for something, the girl said, only she didn't say what. I hope it was trouble they was after. They'll be finding plenty of that here, that's for sure.

All this is going through me head and I ain't taking notice of much else, so it brings me up a bit sharpish when I come to the bridge and turn into me little hideaway and I see that there's somebody there.

He's bent over with his back towards me, looking through me belongings. He don't hear me come in. I watch him for a bit. I know him. He's from one of them gangs live a couple of miles away down the canal. He's been here before on the scrounge. Most likely he's been here when I've been away and all, like now. I've noticed stuff has gone missing before. Only this time I've come back early and caught him at it.

I wait a bit longer till he's took himself a pair of boots off the pile, then I say, 'What you doing here?'

He turns round, sees me, then makes a dash for it, hoping I'm too slow to stop him. I grab him by his collar as he's trying to get past and drag him back and pull his face up close.

'Hallo, Schyte,' I say. 'Dropped in for a chat, have you?'

He knows it ain't no good him trying to struggle or break free. I'm pretty strong for me age, and he's only a scrawny scrap of next-to-nothing, so he just kind of hangs there and grins at me and says, 'I was waiting for you. I come to see if you got anything to eat.'

'Hungry, are you?' I say, and he nods, and I say, 'You won't get far trying to eat through them boots.'

He looks down at the boots he's got, one in each hand, like he don't know how they come there, and drops them. He looks up and gives me that crooked grin again.

118

'I wasn't doing nothing,' he says.

'You were nicking them boots,' I says.

'I wasn't nicking them,' he says. 'I just picked them up. You know how it is. You just pick things up.'

'You were running off with them,' I say. 'You seen me and you tried to run off with them.'

'I never,' he says. 'I never run off. I run, that's all. I just run. You know how it is.'

Yeah, I know how it is. These kids, these gangs. All over the place, they are. Every part of the city you go to there's some gang got it took over, holding its little piece of territory and fighting with the other gangs that are holding their little pieces of territory. A street or two maybe, or a bombed-out building, and sometimes it ain't no more than a tiny patch of dirt and rubble wouldn't no rat call home. But it's their territory and they hold it and it's bad news for you if you go stepping on it and you ain't one of them. It ain't nothing out of the ordinary. I've seen it before, in other cities. It's what happens when the war comes. Things break down and the gangs take over. Scraps and shavings of Nobodies becoming Somebody for a day or two, strutting their bit in the sun and making like they're the best since sliced white and the new world order, whatever they was. When the truth is they're just Kings of the Shitpile, shadows and dust. That's what it all comes down to in the end. Shadows and dust and ashes, and a cold wind blowing through your bones.

I've let him go by now and while all this is going through me head he's going through me stock of food, looking for something with a label on it, I suppose, but them tins ain't got no labels, none of them, and he holds one up and turns to me and says, 'What's in this?'

'Open it and find out,' I say. 'Then you can eat it.'

'What if I don't like it?' he says.

'You're hungry, ain't you?' I say. 'You'll like it.'

I throw him me tin-opener and he opens the tin and looks at what's in it. Then he looks at me again.

'I can see it,' he says, 'and I still don't know what it is.'

I go over and take a look.

'Where was you dragged up, Schyte?' I say. 'You don't know what nothing is unless it's beans. That's artichokes, is what that is,' I tell him.

'Arty what?' he says.

'Artichokes,' I say.

'What's artichokes?' he says.

'That is,' I say.

He sniffs at them.

'Is it some kind of fish?' he says.

'No,' I say. 'It's some kind of vegetable. Eat it. It's good for you.'

Not that I know nor care if it's good for him or not. But I want to find out something from him and the only way to do that is keep him here for a while and keep him happy. There's a small ledge sticks out of the wall of the tunnel low down, and he sits on that and starts eating, picking the artichokes out of the tin and stuffing them in his mouth. I sit meself down on the ledge in the opposite wall and watch him for a bit, and then I ask him about how his nose come to be like it is, which is swollen to twice its size, split and squashed crooked, and it and his face all around it bruised almost black. It's the reason he's been talking even more funny than usual.

'Looks like you been in the wars,' I say.

He touches his nose and sniffs and starts telling me how they had a run-in with the other gang a few days back, and they, meaning his gang, come off worse. And it wasn't fair, he says, cos they, meaning the other gang, must have had some kind of special weapon or power or something, cos they come at them like they was a pack of devils, and his gang didn't have no chance. And on top of all that, he says, somebody from the other gang killed somebody from his gang, which ain't never happened before, and Akh, that's the boss of his gang, it was his best mate as was killed. And the gloves are off now, it's gonna be total and all-out war, but first they got to find out what this special power is the other gang have got, and do something about it, then they'll be for it, good and proper.

I let him go on like this, which he does, all the time eating them artichokes out of the tin. When he's ate the last of them he drinks the liquid and drops the tin on the floor so that it rolls across towards me. I reach out and pick it up and set it down straight. I like to keep things tidy. Now that I've let him have his say, it's time to get round to what I want to try and find out.

'You come across anybody new over that way?' I ask him.

He looks at me and I can tell that he's on his guard straight off.

'Like who?' he says.

'A couple of kids, about your age,' I say.

'I ain't no kid,' he says.

'All right,' I say. 'They wasn't kids and they was about your age. I helped them get into the city a few days ago. They said they had some kind of business here. Didn't say what. They went off along the canal.'

'The canal ain't our territory,' he says.

I could leave it there. I ain't going to get much out of him, even if he does know something. But like I say, I can't get them two out of my head. Him especially. It's like he's got some kind of connection with me, and not just me, with everything. Like he's part of something and I'm part of it as well. Even Schyte. So I don't leave it, and I say to him, 'You might've come across them, though. A boy and a girl.'

'What did she look like?' he says, and I notice he didn't ask what the boy looked like, just her. So I tell him, and I can see it strikes something in him, but he just shakes his head and says, 'I ain't seen her.' Then he adds, 'Nor him.'

'How do you know you ain't seen him?' I say. 'I didn't tell you nothing about him.'

His eyes give a flicker and he knows he's made a mistake, but he covers it and says, 'Tell me about him, then.'

So I start to try and tell him, and it's only then that I realize I can't remember nothing of what he looked like at all. When I try and picture him he's just a shadow, a shadow in the shadows. I remember him being here, sitting where Schyte is now, but the harder I try to see him the more he just kind of melts into the darkness, and he's gone, mist on the water, drifting away.

'He's hard to describe,' I say. 'Ordinary-looking. Like anybody you might see.'

'Nothing special about him, then,' says Schyte.

'Not in his looks,' I say. 'But there was something else—something about him—'

I stop. I don't know what it is I'm trying to say. Schyte's looking at me, waiting for me to go on, and I can see that he's interested only he's trying to let on he ain't, and that puts me on me guard. I remember the dead crow hanging from the tree.

'I don't know what I'm telling you for,' I say. 'You ain't seen him nor the girl, so it don't matter. They was a couple of strangers, that's all. Probably won't see them again. Probably won't nobody will.'

'Yeah,' says Schyte, and he stands up. Then he says, 'Can I have them boots?'

'Them boots you was trying to make off with?' I say.

'I wasn't making off with them,' he says. 'I told you.'

'So you did,' I say. 'But you want them all the same.'

123

'You got lots of boots,' he says.

'For trade,' I say. 'Your lot don't deal in boots, do they? It's scrap, your thing, ain't it? So what do you want them boots for?'

'For me feet,' he says. 'Look.'

I look at his feet. I wish I hadn't. And I think to meself, it won't do no harm him having them. They'll most likely be blown off his feet again in a day or two. And his feet blown off with them.

'Go on, then,' I say.

'Ta,' he says, and goes over to where they're laying on the floor and shoves his feet into them.

'All right?' I ask him.

'A bit tight,' he says.

'You'll get used to them,' I say.

'Yeah,' he says. 'See you round.'

No you won't, I say to meself as he goes off along the canal. I know what's coming, and maybe I should've told him, but even if I had it wouldn't have made any difference, it wouldn't have helped him in any way. He can't escape it, not him nor any of them. It's coming and they ain't got nowhere to go. I have though. As soon as the war's done with this place, it'll be moving on, and me along with it. I've got to make ready for that, get me belongings together, find somewhere safe till it's all over.

I step out of me hideaway and stand there under the bridge looking along the canal. The way I've come it runs towards the city wall, but before it gets there it stops and opens out into a kind of basin. It used to be full of water, I suppose, but it's mostly just sludge now. Anyway, one side of this basin there's a wall and an opening in the wall and steps going down to the tunnel where I get in and out of the city. It ain't going to be much good hiding out down there on account as it don't go down very far and comes up just the other side of the wall, and there could be trouble out there once everything gets started. It could cave in, and all, if a shell was to drop on it. But there's another tunnel I found, going off from the first one, and that goes deeper and runs all the way to the river and that's where it comes up. It's all blocked with rubble where it starts to run under the wall, rocks and stones packed in tight, and I reckon the soldiers must've done that when they first come to stop anybody getting out. But the shelling's broke it loose and there's a place I can crawl through. That's where I'm going, down there deep under the wall. Take a few supplies, get meself stowed away snug and tight, and wait for it to be over. Then make me way out and move on.

I look up the canal the other way. The sun's low but still bright, and there's a smoky tang in the air. Everything's still. It'll be evening soon. Then something flickers in the corner of me eye and I turn quickly, but there ain't nothing, just a shadow, and when I look it's gone. I shiver in the cold. I got things to do. I go back inside to start getting ready.

Troggs: Ik

He's made this kind of dummy.

It's up there on top of the scrap-pile, standing straight with its arms stretched out. It ain't got no head.

He made it three days ago, the day after the fight. Started making it. He keeps changing it, pulling bits off it, sticking new bits on, like he can't get it right.

I suppose when he gets it right, that's when he'll put the head on.

Hey, Joey, I say. He don't look at me. Hey, Crowboy, I say, and this time he turns his head and looks down towards me. I'm standing at the bottom of the scrap-pile.

He grins. Maybe he likes the name.

What is that thing? I say.

A puzzled look comes on his face like he don't know himself what it is.

Has it got a name? I ask him.

He looks back at it, then looks at me again.

It's not finished yet, is all he says, then he turns back to what he was doing.

He's drilling a hole through a jagged piece of rusty metal, looks like it was part of an oil-drum once. Lots of old oil-drums lying around here. It ain't easy cos it's only an old drill he's found among the scrap and probably wasn't ever meant to go through metal. He keeps at it though.

What it is, this dummy, is just a length of tubing stuck upright and another shorter piece of tubing tied across it with some scraps of rope. He found a couple of sacks and ripped them open and hung them on the piece that goes across. He done all that on the first day.

The next day he found the drill started drilling holes in things and tying them on to the sacking.

First he put on an old kettle. Then a saucepan lid. He spent all the day drilling holes in different things off the scrap-pile and tying them on. But he was never satisfied. He'd stop and look, then take a piece off and throw it away. Then he'd find something else, drill a hole in that, and tie it on.

All day yesterday and all today, doing the same thing. Trying to make it so it looks just right. If I knew what that was I'd go and help him. But I bet he don't even know himself. That's why he's having such a hard time getting it done.

There's nobody else here, only me and him. When he first started some of the others come to watch. Nasty and Ell and Yass and Uba and Lex. I come across as well but they told me to piss off so I went away. I watched from a distance.

They called up to him and asked him what he was

doing but he didn't take no notice of them. They called up a few more times. I knew if he didn't answer they'd stop acting friendly. He did say something to them then and Lex said something back to him and they all laughed.

I don't know why it came to me then, but it did. Hearing them laugh. The sound of it. It came to me that they were afraid of him. Like they're afraid of me. Because of what I told them. But I don't know why they should be afraid of him.

They went away not long after. I came back across and sat down and watched him. I've been here ever since.

There's nobody else here. The others haven't come back. Even Mal ain't here. I don't know where she's gone. Kazz is down by the canal, sitting on the lock-gate, looking down into the water. It's just me and him.

He's finished drilling the hole. He takes a piece of string and runs it through. Then he lifts it up and ties the string to one of the arms so the piece of metal hangs down. It clinks against the lid that's hanging next to it. The whole dummy-figure tilts a bit to one side, and all the metal that's tied to it clinks and rattles. Some of it catches the sunlight and flashes. Like it's sending out some kind of signal.

The kind of signal nobody knows what it means. And even if they did, there ain't nobody out there to see it.

Joey

he will come when it is finished when I have it right
he will come he will shine   body of light feathers of
flame   as I saw him they will see him in the burning
and the shining   he spoke to me the words   here is
where I shall come   I did not see him only heard him
here I shall be revealed   the words him speaking them
inside me   all shall see me shining in human form   I
asked him what form   it shall be known   and I began
to make it what I'm making now   his body to shine his
wings to flash   the fire the burning the light the flame
when it's ready he'll come down   as when he came
down before   out of the glass the coloured window
out of the burning and the voices   the screaming the
screaming then the silence   in the silence he came   but
first I've got to fix it   and he shall come   to get it right
in the light and the shining   when it's finished   then it
shall be known

Troggs: Ik

It reminds me of something I seen when I was a boy.

There used to be fields outside the city down by the river. They grew stuff down there. I think it was cabbages. Perhaps not all the time. Sometimes it was. This one time it was cabbages.

Me and Kazz went out there like we did sometimes. She was little then and I had to look after her. She was always running off somewhere. She'd see something, or get an idea in her head about something, and just go running off. I had to make sure she didn't get herself lost.

We came down to the edge of the fields.

There's a man in the fields, Kazz said.

I looked. I told her it wasn't a man, it was a scarecrow. It was there to keep the birds off the field. It wasn't doing a very good job. The field was full of crows.

Before I could stop her Kazz went running into the field, shouting out and waving her arms. The crows went flying up, but they didn't fly away. They just flew up and circled around for a bit, then came down again.

Some of them came down on the scarecrow. They sat on its arms and on its head and they started pecking at it, pulling it to pieces with their beaks. Kazz started to shout at them.

Stop it, she shouted. Stop it, crows. You're hurting him.

She turned to me.

Make them stop, she said.

I told her again it was only a scarecrow.

But she'd put the idea in my head. It seemed to me it was a man. Or it had been once, and all that was left of him was a few sticks and scraps of rag, after the crows had finished with him.

That's what that dummy Joey's making reminds me of. That scarecrow. Something that was a man once and ain't no more.

Or maybe something that ain't a man yet.

It comes to the same thing.

And it's how I feel too. Like something that's just rags and sticks, something the crows have tore to pieces. Ever since I seen Rok dead. Ever since I told them I seen him dead.

They look at me like that. The others. Lex and Nasty and Yass and Ell and Uba. Like I'm something ain't human no more. Even Ekt keeps his distance. I can tell he don't want nothing to do with me. They all wish I wasn't here.

Cos they know what I told them was true.

And it ain't a matter of the one who did it not wanting to be found out.

It ain't a matter of that one being protected by the others.

It ain't even a matter of who it was that did it.

I've thought about this a lot. Sitting here, watching Joey build his scarecrow, I think I've got it figured out.

It don't matter who did it because we all did it.

We all held that that knife.

We all pushed the knife into his gut.

We all ran and left him there, bleeding, dying.

We're the killers. All of us.

Cos we're all part of the same thing. And the war's part of it too. It ain't something outside us. It's part of us, and we're part of it, and there ain't no difference between us and it.

That's what I know. That's what I told them. That's why they wish I wasn't here.

And that's why he's building his scarecrow. Up there, on top of the scrap-heap, working at it, trying to get it right. It isn't just something he's doing cos he feels like it. It means something. Like the doll he gave to Kazz and she gave to Ekt. He tied crow feathers to it. He made it mean something. Kazz could see what it meant, and I think I can see what this scarecrow means. What it's for.

It's to keep the crows away. The birds of death.

He calls down to me.

Hey, he says. Look.

He gives the scarecrow a little push. It moves, and that sets off all the pieces of metal moving as well, rattling and clanking. The sound echoes across the wasteground.

It's nearly ready, he says. Then something strange.

He'll come when it's finished.

Who will, I ask him.

He doesn't answer my question. Instead he says, It will be finished soon.

Then he starts rummaging again through the scrap.

Over on the other side of the canal Ekt comes out of headquarters and walks up towards the lock-gate. Kazz is still sitting there.

She's still looking into the water.

Kazz

I'm looking into the water and it's dark but sometimes there are streaks of red, little tails of flame, they flicker in my eyes and through my eyes, light and dark, looking down into the water and out of the water and then it becomes a face.

This is my face in the water floating with the eyes looking through the light and the dark, and there the little flames twist and flicker through my face, and my face in the water twists and flickers, it won't keep still, so it's my face and not my face, and then not my face but some other.

The other face in the water, it looks out of the water, through the light and the dark, the face inside my face, then my face inside the other face, that face and my face twisting together, then pulling free, then there is only the other face.

Its mouth moves, it's trying to speak, to say something, the mouth twisting, but no sound only twists of flame flickering, and my mouth moves too, and then his words are there, I speak them and they burn and I see them burning.

You killed me. You must tell them. I'm here. You must show them. Tell them, show them, you killed me, I'm here.

And the face floats and the mouth speaks the words I speak them.

Troggs: Ik

What's it all mean, then?

It's Lex, standing behind him. I didn't see him. Like he's come from nowhere.

What? I say.

That, he says. He's looking up at Joey and his scarecrow on top of the scrap-heap.

I don't know, I say.

Maybe just a load of junk, he says.

I shrug, and look back to the canal. Ekt is standing next to Kazz. She's still sitting on the lock-gate and she's talking to him. She points at the water.

Something going on? says Lex. He's looking as well. Looks like there's something going on, he says.

I look back up to the top of the scrap-heap. Joey's putting something on top of the scarecrow. It's an upturned can, the kind they used to put petrol in, when there used to be petrol. The scarecrow's got a head now. He's finished it.

Ekt is kneeling down now, looking into the water where Kazz is pointing. He gives a start, sits back. Then he stands up.

What you think it is? says Lex.

I don't know, I say.

You don't know much, do you? he says.

I know something, I say.

He looks at me. He knows what I mean.

You're gonna know something else in a minute, he says.

What? I say.

They're coming over, he says.

He looks back towards the canal. I look as well, and there's Ekt and Kazz walking towards us, and it looks serious.

Mal

I'm standing watch at the edge of the territory and I'm freezing cold. I've been here all afternoon, and even though the sun's bright, the air's bitter, and the frost hasn't lifted off the ground. Somebody should come along soon and take over. I hope they hurry up.

Behind me there are some old factories, most with their roofs blown in. In front there's a street with a few derelict houses, and where the street ends a large expanse of wasteground opens up. All that's Geek territory. There's no one moving out there. I haven't seen anybody all the time I've been here. I didn't see anybody yesterday, either, nor the day before.

I'm beginning to think maybe they've gone. Maybe we hit them so hard they just packed up and moved out. I said this to Lex this morning. He shook his head and laughed, like I'd said something funny. His eyes didn't laugh, though.

'You don't know the Geeks,' he said. 'They haven't gone nowhere. They've hit us hard in the past and we didn't go. We just waited, then hit them back. They're

141

no different to us. They'll do the same. So you just do your job and keep watch.'

I found out from the others that Lex and Ekt are brothers. It was them that started the gang, just after the war started. I asked them who was here first, them or the Geeks, and nobody seemed to know for certain. Some said they were here first, some said the Geeks. They couldn't really remember. It's like it all happened a long time ago, it's some old story from way back in the past. Sometimes that's how I feel about things. As if all that's happened, and all that's happening now, it's just a story that somebody's telling me. But I'm listening to it and I'm in it at the same time. We're all of us in it, all part of the same story.

Except Joey. He's got his own story.

And Kazz. The others don't seem to like her much. They seem a bit afraid of her as well. Ekt's the only one who isn't. There's something between the two of them. Something that happened once that brought the two of them together, and now it holds them together and it won't let them go. And keeps other people out. Maybe that's why the others don't like her. Maybe that's why Lex looks at her the way he does.

There's this way he has of looking sometimes. A light comes into his eyes, a hard cold light. Even when he's being friendly. Especially when he's being friendly. Like there's something watching you from a long way off. Something that isn't Lex.

That's how he looks at Kazz. And that's how he looks at Joey as well.

I saw it when we were standing round the scrap and Joey had started making that figure. He'd stood the upright piece in the top of the pile, and was tying the cross-piece onto it.

'What's he doing?' said Ell.

'Looks like he's making something,' said Uba.

'I'm glad you told us that, Uba,' said Nasty. 'Only if you hadn't, I might've thought he was doing a dance.'

'You couldn't do a dance up there,' said Uba. 'You'd fall off.'

'Like you did,' said Nasty. 'Fell off your perch and you ain't been right since.'

Yass laughed.

'Fell off his perch,' he said. 'That's good, that is.' He couldn't stop laughing, like Nasty had said something funny. 'Right on top of his head.'

'Leave it out, Nasty,' said Ell. 'He ain't done nothing to you.'

'Except just be here,' said Nasty.

They're always going on like that. Nasty makes fun of Uba and Ell sticks up for him. Then Ell makes fun of Uba and Nasty sticks up for him. Sometimes Yass joins in, taking sides with Nasty, and then with Ell. But it's always Uba they make fun of. He doesn't seem to mind. Or maybe he just doesn't know. But hearing them go on like that makes me feel good. It's how we used to talk to each other back home, before the war came. When things were ordinary and you thought they'd always be like that.

Joey finished tying the cross-piece to the upright pole and he stood back and looked at it.

'So what is it, then?' said Ell. She said it to me.

'I don't know,' I said. 'It's just something he's making.'

'What for?' said Uba.

'I don't know,' I said again. 'He just makes things.'

I told them about the time we were coming through the mountains and we came across some bones lying among the rocks. The bones of some animal. He took one of them and made some holes in it with a sharp stone and blew into it. It made a sound, a thin, high-pitched note. It sounded strange and eerie up there in the mountains. He blew it again and there came this scream from the sky. We looked up and saw a large bird, a hawk of some kind, circling overhead. It screamed once more and then floated away out of sight.

'You trying to say he called the bird with that flute he made?' said Yass.

'I'm not trying to say anything,' I said. 'I'm just saying what happened.'

All this time we'd been talking Lex hadn't been saying anything. Just standing there listening, and watching Joey. He'd found a couple of sacks and was emptying scrap metal out of them. Then he started ripping the sacks open.

'What you reckon he's doing now?' Ell said to me.

Before I could answer, Lex said, 'She don't know. But he does. He knows what he's doing.' He looked at me. 'That's right, ain't it?' he said.

'Yes,' I said. 'I suppose he does.'

'He knows, right enough,' said Lex, and he grinned, and that's when I saw it in his eyes, that cold hard light coming from a long way off, that thing that wasn't Lex looking out at Joey and looking out at me.

Something like the scream of that hawk in the mountains. Nothing human about it at all.

I put down my weapon, that rusty piece of railing I took with me into the fight, and shove my hands in the pockets of my trousers. They're hurting with the cold and the end of my fingers are numb. I walk up and down a bit to try and get warm, and as I do, out of the corner of my eye I see something move. At first I think it's someone come to take over, but then I realize it can't be because the movement came from across the street, where the derelict houses are. Straight off I grab my weapon and stare out across the street, at every house, and at the gullies that run between the houses. There's nothing. The empty windows stare back at me, the blank doorways gape. Perhaps it was just a rat. Perhaps just the light.

Then there's another movement, and footsteps, from behind me this time, and I turn, and there's Ell and Uba coming towards me and I raise my hand and just then something hits the side of my head and there's a sharp pain and when I put my hand to my face there's blood.

Geeks: Schyte

The tricky bit is coming up out from between the factories and getting across the road to the houses cos it's open there ain't it and sometimes they have somebody on watch. And sure enough they have, only I'm in luck cos they ain't looking my way, so I nip out sharpish and get myself through a doorway and inside before whoever it is sees me. It's easy from here cos all I got to do now is go out the back and I'm home. I'm thinking I'd better get a shift on and all, get back and tell Akh what I found out from the old man about them two strangers, one of them's that girl but the other one, the boy he told about, we ain't seen him, he never come to fight and I wonder why that is. I hang on a bit though cos these boots am killing me feet, I told the old man they was too small, but he wasn't going to change his mind, was he, and let me have another pair. One of these days I'm gonna go back there, take a couple of the others with me, Fig and Jax maybe, and we'll do him over, take all his stuff, all them tins of food and all them pairs of boots he's got, and maybe I'll get meself his coat and all, and I won't be so cold then, least not so cold as I am now. So anyway I take the boots off and me feet am all red and throbbing and I give them a bit of a rub, and then I put them back on again and I decide to take a look and see who it is they've got on watch, and I take a look through the window and it's her ain't it, that girl, the new recruit, her that smashed me nose, I'd know her anywhere. Her's looking out across the street like maybe her thought her heard or seen something but her don't know I'm here or her'd be looking this way and her ain't. Down by me feet there's a piece a broken brick so I reach down and pick it up and I reckon I can get a clear shot through the window so I take aim and just then two more come out from between the factories, it's Ell and Uba, but I ain't gonna stop now cos me arm's already starting to move and I think to meself, What the hell, here's one for you, and I let fly and bullseye it smacks her right in the face, a real beauty. I ought to go now, make tracks, but I can't help it, I have to stay a bit see what happens, and there's Ell and Uba looking across to see if they can see who done it and I can hear them arguing. Uba wants to come over and I think, Yeah, come on Uba, let's have you, and he's coming but Ell pulls him back, then her says something to her I hit with the brick, her face is all bleeding, ain't it, and that makes me feel really good, so I just can't help grinning. And I'm grinning right into Uba's face, he's seen me and he knows it's me grinning at him, so I give him a wave, let him know I've seen him, then I duck down and I'm off, but I ain't got far when somebody grabs me by the throat.

Mal

My face is cut, and though it's not deep, it hurts, and it's bleeding a lot. Ell's given me a piece of rag to press against it. Uba wants to go across the street and get whoever it was who threw the stone. Ell holds him back, tells him not to be thick. It could be a trap. They start arguing. I don't hear much of what they're saying. My face feels like it's on fire and I press the rag hard against the wound, pushing it deep into the pain. Suddenly I realize that Ell's speaking to me, asking me how I am. I tell her I'm OK, though I'm not. I feel a bit sick and everything keeps going far away and coming back again.

I can hear Uba speaking, very loud.

'It's Schyte!'

'Where?' says Ell.

'There,' says Uba. 'In that window.'

'I can't see anything.'

'He's gone now,' says Uba. 'But I seen him. He was grinning at me out that window.'

They carry on talking but their words fly away. Everything flies away except the knot in my stomach, and that's growing tighter and tighter. I'm thinking it can't get any tighter or it'll burst, when that's just what it does. The whole knot just bursts, and I throw up.

I double up, clutching myself, hot tears streaming down my face. My legs give way and I slump down onto the ground, put my head between my knees, and breathe in and out deeply, trying to make it go away. I'm shaking, my body aches, and where there was a knot in my stomach now there's just a kind of emptiness that grows and shrinks and grows again, wrenching at my insides.

Then a roaring noise comes from far off, getting closer, until it's all around me and inside me.

I try to hold on to something but there's nothing to grip, my hands are scrabbling in air, and I'm falling and everything's broken into pieces, smashed fragments of glass flying apart. There are voices screaming, and flames, and faces in the flames, and suddenly I know where I am.

The church is burning. The soldiers are standing in front of the burning church. They're not looking at me. They're looking at Joey. He's coming out of the church. He's coming out of the burning church and it's in his arms. He's coming towards me carrying it in his arms. The church is burning and he's carrying it towards me. I know what it is and I don't want to see it. He keeps on coming towards me and I don't want to see it.

I try to cry out. If I can cry out he'll go away and it will all go away and I won't have to see it. But the cry's stuck in my throat like a stone, a lump of black stone in my throat. It won't come out and he's coming towards me with the burning church behind him and the soldiers. Now he stops in front of me. He's holding it out towards me. I have to look. I'm going to see it. He holds it in his arms out towards me and now it comes free, I spit it out, the black stone cry, it comes long and loud, tearing my throat. Then I'm sitting on the ground.

I look up. There are the houses across the street. There's the sky just beginning to grow dark above them. My face is wet. I wipe it with my hand and look at my hand. Blood and dirt and tears. I wipe my hand on my trousers. My breathing's easier. It's all right now. It's passed. I didn't see it. I'm all right.

There are voices talking.

'You should've let me go after him.'

'You'd never have caught him.'

'I'd like to have tried.'

'It wasn't worth it.'

I know the voices. Ell and Uba. But now there's another voice, coming from further off.

'You're right. Wasn't nobody there.'

I know that voice too. I've heard it before, but I can't give it a name. Ell and Uba are speaking again.

'Where'd you come from?'

'I never seen you.'

'You been over there?'

The third voice speaks again, closer now.

'Yeah. Just looking around.'

'You didn't see nothing?'

'No.'

'He must've scarpered.'

'He might've been hiding.'

'Who?'

'Schyte.'

'It was him did that?'

'Yeah.'

'He wasn't there. Like you said, he must've scarpered.'

'I'd like to get hold of that Schyte.'

'You'll get your chance.'

The voice floats in and out. A face starts to appear, a name attached to it, then fades again, becomes a shadow. Yass? No, not Yass.

Suddenly it's loud and sharp and clear.

'She all right?'

'I reckon so. It's just a cut.' That's Ell.

'She throwed up.' Uba.

'Maybe she ain't as tough as we thought.' Ell again.

'She's tough.' That's the voice I can't place. 'You seen her the other night.'

'I seen her, yeah.' That's Uba. 'I seen her bust Schyte in the face. Smashed it wide open. I reckon that's why he chucked that stone.'

I bust Schyte in the face. Those words don't mean anything. Who's Schyte? The one who threw the stone.

But I don't know him. I don't remember smashing any-body's face open.

'How you doing?' It's that other voice again. The name's almost there but it keeps slipping away from me. 'Can you stand up? Here, I'll help you.'

A hand under my arm. I rise to my feet, turn to see who it is.

'OK now?'

The voice speaking to me. I see the face with the voice coming out of it. The voice and the face go together and give themselves a name. Lex.

I speak to him, to Lex. 'Yes, I'm OK,' I say. There's a bitter taste in my mouth. 'I don't know what happened. Just went a bit funny.'

'It can get you like that sometimes,' he says.

'I'll get back,' I say. 'Maybe I'll feel better after a rest.'

'We've all got to be getting back,' says Lex, 'but we won't be having no rest.'

'What you mean?' says Ell. 'We've only just got here.'

'Ekt wants everybody back at headquarters,' says Lex.

'What for,' says Uba.

'You'll find out when you get there,' says Lex.

'What about keeping watch?' says Ell.

'What about obeying orders?' says Lex. 'Move.'

Ell and Uba move off the way they came, down the passageway between the factories. I follow them. Lex walks next to me. I get the feeling he's hanging back on purpose, that there's something he wants to say.

But he doesn't say anything, and we just keep walking between the factories then out onto the open ground that runs down to the canal.

My feet crunch on the hard earth. The cold evening air bites into the cut on my face. I can feel how my face is starting to swell. My throat's dry and my eyes are smarting. But it's all real, all ordinary, here and now, and I'm glad of it.

Ell and Uba are at the towpath now, turning right towards the lock-gate, which is where we cross over to the warehouse. We're quite a way behind them. Lex suddenly says, 'What do you think of what Ik said?'

'Said about what?' I say, even though I know.

'About one of theirs being killed in the fight,' he says. 'What do you make of it?'

'I don't know,' I say.

'You didn't see anything?' he says.

'If I did I don't remember,' I say. 'I don't remember anything about the fight.'

He doesn't say anything for a while and we walk on. He keeps his head lowered, looking at the ground. Then he says, 'This mate of yours. Joey. The Crowboy. Is he for real?'

I don't know how to answer that. I spent months travelling with him, across the plains, through the mountains. He led the way and I followed him, and I don't know why. I don't know who he is, or what he is, not even his name. It was me called him Joey. But sometimes it seems he's the only thing that is for real. Though not in the way I think Lex means it.

'Yes,' I say. 'He's for real.'

'Good,' says Lex. 'Cos if what Ik said is true, we're in big trouble, and we're going to need all the help we can get.'

He lifts his head now, turns his face towards me and smiles. I meet his eyes.

Something looks out at me from a long way off.

Troggs: Ekt

Everybody here? OK. Listen. I got something to tell you. We've found a body in the canal. Kazz seen it and she showed it to me. It looks like it's been there a few days. It's Rok. Rok's body. And he didn't drown. Somebody stabbed him. Then his body was dumped in the canal. I reckon it was the Geeks that put him there. But it wasn't the Geeks that killed him. It was one of us. So Ik was right all along. One of us killed him when we had the fight. I ain't going to ask who it was, not yet. We can leave that for later. What we got to do now is get ready for the Geeks. They'll be coming after us, and it won't be just to get their goods back. It'll be for revenge. Cos we killed Rok. He was their second-in-command and he was Akh's best mate. So they'll be coming, and it won't be like it's been before. Things have changed. It's us and them, now, a fight to the death. And when it's over there's gonna be only one gang, like there used to be. And we know who that gang's gonna be. Yeah. That's right. Us. Cos we're the best. That's why the Crowboy come here, that's why he come to us and not them. To show us we're the best. And he give us this as a sign.

This doll. Only it ain't just a doll. Like I said, it's a sign. He come and he give us this and we went up against the Geeks and we thrashed them and took their goods. He give us the power. Maybe he even made it so Rok got killed. Maybe that was a sign as well. And now he's give us another sign. Up there on top of the goods. That thing made from the goods we took. Look at it. You know what it's saying. We're here, it says, and we're here to stay. The Geeks are done for, and it's Troggs for ever.

OK. Quiet now. We got to start making ready. They'll be coming soon. Akh won't rest till he's had his revenge. It might be tonight, it might be tomorrow, but it won't be long. And whenever it is we'll let them come and we'll be waiting. So from now on we're all on lookout. Nobody's off-duty. And we got to make sure the Crowboy's safe, see to it he don't get hurt. So for now we'll take him to headquarters, keep him there, put a watch on the door. We can take it in turns. Nasty, Uba, you'll be first. Everybody else will spread out round the territory in pairs. Lex has got places marked out. He'll tell you where to go. Soon as you see them, one of you let the rest of us know. But don't do nothing. Let them come in. Don't do nothing till I give the word. We'll let them come right in, all the way. And once they're in, we've got them. We close in around them so they got no way out. Then we finish them, and we finish them good. Right? Right.

OK. Let's get moving.

Geeks: Schyte

Soon as he's finished talking and they start to break up I'm off down the gully between the factories and out towards the wasteground, and I can't wait till I get back and tell the others, and I'm thinking to meself they'll have to take more notice of me now, pay me a bit of respect for once and no more jokes, cos they all think they'm something, don't they, and I ain't nothing, well they'm going to see now, ain't they, that I can be something and all. That Lex, he thinks he's something, thinks he's clever and got it all worked out, well he ain't so clever as he thinks, he can't be, cos if he was he wouldn't have let me go, would he, but he did, and I bet he never thought I'd have the guts to follow him, well I did, so there, that's all you know, Lex, and there I was right in among them, and they never knowed it, never knowed I was there all the time, close enough to see their faces, and that Crowboy, watching and listening to everything that was said, and now I know and when I tell Akh and the others they'll have to listen to me for once and take some notice. And it ain't before time.

I come out the factories, and there's the street and

the houses across the street, and I stop a bit to get me breath. Right over there is the house I was in when I chucked the brick, so her must've been standing just about where I'm standing now when it hit her, smack in the face, that was good that was, it made me laugh. Mind you, when Lex grabbed hold of me I stopped laughing then, didn't I, I thought I was done for, never seen him coming nor how he got in there. And he looked like he was going to do for me, and all, got that grin, and he was squeezing tight so's I could hardly breathe. What's up, Schyte, he said, ain't a broke nose enough for you, you want me to break your neck and all? Well, course I didn't but I couldn't say nothing, could I, with his hand round me throat squeezing tight, then he pulled me right up close to him and I thought here it comes, only it wasn't what I thought, cos he kneed me in the bollocks and loosed me throat and I just dropped, gasping. Get up, Schyte, he said to me, it can't hurt that much, you ain't got no balls, and he pulled me up to me feet, and then he said, Shall I tell you why I'm going to let you go, and I still couldn't say much on account of I hadn't got no voice, so I just nodded, and he said, I want you to give a message to Akh, that's why. Reckon you can do that, Schyte, reckon you can remember what I'm going to tell you and pass it on? So I nodded again, and then he said to tell Akh that he was finished, Troggs was top gang and Geeks was over and done with, and I couldn't help it, could I, I had to laugh, so I did and he smacked me in the face, and he said, Listen, Schyte, you listen to me good what I'm going to tell you and make sure you don't forget it.

So then he told me how they had somebody with them called Crowboy, and this Crowboy had come along and had a special kind of power, and he'd give this power to the Troggs and it made them stronger than anybody. And all the time he was telling me this I was remembering what the old man told me about that boy and that girl, and wanting to know if I'd seen them. And I was thinking it can't be the girl, her's a good fighter but nothing special about her, so maybe it's the boy, cos the old man had said there was something special about him, and anyway, Lex called him Crowboy not Crowgirl. Then Lex was saying to me, You got all that, and I said, Yeah, I got it, cos I'd had me voice back now. You sure, he said, and I told him, Yeah, I'm sure. You make sure you tell him, then, said Lex, you tell him that as long as we got Crowboy we can't be beat, so you might just as well the lot of you pack up and move on and go and find some other territory, cos we're taking over yours, and if you ain't gone soon we'll be coming over there to take it, and there won't be nothing you can do to stop us.

That's what you think, Lex, only what you didn't count on was me following you and taking a look at this Crowboy for meself, cos I figured that's what I better do, so that's what I did. I went out the house and made it like I was going back, but then I ducked down behind a wall, then I snuck in again after he'd gone, and I watched him go across to Ell and Uba and that girl, and I seen them all go and I waited a bit and then I followed them. Right behind them and they never knowed it, all the way into their territory, and I hid myself down that gully, and seen and heard it all, their whole plan. So now I'm on me way back and trying to keep it all in me head what I found out, and saying to meself, Come on, Schyte, you can do it, this time you ain't gonna get it wrong this time you're gonna get it right.

So here I am at last and there they all am just sitting around the fire, and as soon as they see me Jax says, Look what the cat's brought back, and Dis says, Where you been, Schyte, we thought you'd run off or got caught or something. Missed me, have you, I says, and Little Jax says, Like a boil up the bum, then Akh says, You better tell us what you been up to, so I do. I tell them about what the old man said about the two strangers, and about what Lex said, and how I followed them, and heard their plan, and how I seen the Crowboy, and all, I tell them everything and don't forget nothing, except I keep one thing back, I'm saving that. They all just listen, don't say nothing, and Akh he's got his head down looking at the ground, and he stays like that after I've finished, but all the others am asking me questions, like, Who is he, this Crowboy? and, What kind of power's he got? And, Is some kind of magic? And I say, I don't know.

I'm just telling you what Lex said and what I seen. Then Dis says, Did you see him, and I tell him, Yeah, I did, and Little Jax says, What's he look like, and I say, Nothing special, but he must be, cos they took him to their headquarters and put a guard on him, like I said. And it's only then that Akh looks up and says kind of quiet-like but we all listen, I got a plan.

He tells us his plan. They'm expecting us to go across there and raid them, he says, and get revenge for what they done to Rok. That's what they'm waiting for, so we ain't gonna do it. What we'll do instead is grab this Crowboy of theirs, take him right from under their noses, and bring him back here. Then they'll have to come and try and get him back, and when they do, that's when we'll get them, here on our ground. Well it sounds like a good enough plan to me, but Dis ain't sure, and he says, You heard what Schyte said, they've got him in their headquarters. That's over the other side of the canal. How we going to get across there without them seeing us? I can see by the look on Akh's face that he knowed that was going to be a problem, and he says, There's got to be a way, and that's when I come in and tell them what it is I've been keeping back.

There's a tunnel, I say, down by where the old man lives. Then I tell them how I seen him go down there after I left him, so I went down there and all, and how the main part of it runs down under the city wall, but there's a smaller one, ain't there, that branches off, and that comes up on the other side of the canal. That really gets them, and they all look at me like they ain't never seen me before, and I'm really buzzing now, and I say just to make sure they understand, We can get across to their headquarters, and all we got is the two guards to deal with, then get the Crowboy, and we'm off before they even know it.

Now they'm all patting me on the back and shaking their heads and laughing like they can't believe it's me saved the day for them, and I'm grinning and laughing along with them, and Akh says, You done good today, Schyte, and they all say, Yeah! even Fig. Then I say to her, Maybe you'll lend me your coat now, Fig, so's I won't freeze me arse off, and her looks at me and I think I know what her's going to say, but her don't, instead her says, Yeah, when all this over, I will, yeah.

Troggs: Lex

It's going well. Better than I thought. Running into Schyte like that was a bit of luck. Funny sometimes, you start planning something and suddenly everything just starts falling into place. Like all you got to do is stand back and let it happen. Like it's been waiting to happen all this time. All it needed was you to come along and start it off. And it's happening now, all right. Even if I wanted to I couldn't stop it. Not that I want to. It's rolling, on the move, rolling right down to the end. Let it roll, bring it on.

Black down there. The water. Cold, and all. Ice on surface. Break it, this stone. Like that. Now it's gone, down to the bottom. Where he is. Them big stones we tied to him so he'd sink. Don't want him coming up again. I bet he's cold down there. White, his face. Whiter than I ever seen anything. Not even dead. Less than dead. Nothing. I never had nothing against him. We used to get on.

It's cold up here, and all. Hands are freezing. And my feet. Hardly feel them. Do something to keep warm. Move about. Stamp my feet. Blow on my hands. Clap them together. A bit of feeling now. Better.

It's his own fault, Ekt. He started all this. We had a good gang, till he brought her back with him. She saved his life, OK. But she wasn't the gang. Never has been never will be. Just full of crazy talk. And he listens to her like it means something. It don't mean nothing. Everybody knows it but him. It's me he should've been listening to. Get rid of her. I told him. Get rid of her. But he wouldn't. He knows best. So the gang split like I said it would. And now here's this Crowboy come along. Another crazy. As if one wasn't enough. And still he don't listen. Only to the crazies. The rest of them as well, now. There's only me got any sense left. So just me to do something about it. End it. End it now, tonight. Have one gang again. One boss. That's the way it ought to be. The way it's gonna be.

Nasty and Uba over there. Outside the door. On guard. Keeping him safe. Who's that? Walking up and down, flapping his arms. Uba. Nasty just standing there. Telling him to keep still. Uba telling him to shut up. Nasty comes back with something. Uba comes back with something else. How it always is. Nothing ever any different. But it will be tonight. I could just go straight over the lock, round the back to the door. They wouldn't think nothing. But I'd have to take them both at once. And I ain't sure of that. Even with the knife. They'll make a racket, bring the others. It's got to be done quiet. One at a time. Nothing for it, then. In the water, here. Come out further down. Go round the back way. I wonder which one it'll be first? It don't matter really.

Won't be many of us left by the time it's finished. Not many of them either, but that's OK. There's plenty more where they come from. Head up into the city, a raiding party, take a few captives. It won't take long to build up numbers again.

They'll be coming soon. Once Schyte tells them what he heard. They'll be up for it, want to get in first, put one over on us. Smash and grab. Or just do him in. Either way it don't make no difference. I wonder how they'll get across? No need to worry about that, they'll find some way or other. Don't have to plan for everything. Take the chances as they come. Make it up as you go along, see what happens. Once you get something started, it works itself out. That's what gives you the buzz. And that's what it's all about. The jump. The buzz. The kick. So let's get it done.

Ease myself down. Crack the ice with my boot. Slide in. Freezing water. Right through. To the bone.

I'll tell them I tried to stop them and they threw me in.

Go down and say hello to Rok. How you doing, mate? Feeling lonely? Don't worry, you'll soon have company.

Up. And out.

Troggs: Ik

We're on watch just up from the lock in-between two of the old factories. We can see the lock and the head-quarters over the canal.

If they come down that way we'll see them but they won't see us. Then I'll go and tell the others like Ekt said. That's what we decided, me and Mal.

But we've been here hours and we haven't seen them yet.

Maybe they ain't coming tonight.

I'm froze.

I don't think they're coming.

Time passes slow.

Mal isn't saying a lot. She's looking out most the time but she's not looking out for them. She's thinking about Joey being over there in headquarters without her. She ain't happy about it.

His scarecrow's out there lit up by the moon. Up there on top of the scrap-pile all shiny. Like it's keeping watch as well. All it is is a lot of bits and pieces of scrap put together. I know that. I watched him make it. But some-how it's more than that. Somehow it makes me feel safe.

Safe as houses.

That's what Mom used to say when we were little. When it came to bedtime I didn't want the light off because I was frightened of the dark. Kazz wasn't, even though she's younger. Just me.

There's nothing to be frightened of, Mom said. We're safe here. Safe as houses.

She said that even after the war came.

We'll be all right. We're safe. Safe as houses.

In my experience houses ain't that safe. They ain't safe at all.

I don't like thinking about that and here I am thinking about it when Mal suddenly turns to me.

What is it with Kazz and Ekt? she says.

What you mean? I say.

There's something between them, she says. Then she says, Like with me and Joey.

I don't say anything for a bit. I don't really want to talk about it. And the thing is as well I don't know everything about it cos I wasn't there. Ekt's never said much. And whatever Kazz says you got to take it apart and try and put it back together again so's it makes some kind of sense.

You don't have to tell me, she says.

I don't mind, I say, and I tell her what I know.

I tell her how it was after the war had come and they were shelling the city. They shelled us most nights but there was one night it was really bad. Me and Kazz lived with Mom and Dad then. They were at home but I wasn't. I'd gone out to look for food. There wasn't much to be had, and you had to scrounge or beg or scrat around for what you could get. That's what I was doing.

Then I tell her how when it started I tried to get back home but I couldn't. Shells were falling everywhere, houses, buildings, streets, they was all going up in smoke and dust and flames. It was like the whole city was burning. I knew if I stayed out in it I'd be killed. I had to find somewhere to shelter. So I ducked down into the cellar of a house that had been shelled before and stayed there. I hoped it wouldn't get shelled again.

It lasted all night, I tell her. When morning come and the shelling stopped I went home. But it wasn't there. Not just our house, the whole street. Nor any of the streets around it. They was all gone. Nothing left but rubble and smoke.

I stayed around. I didn't know what for, there wasn't anything for me there. Nothing left of my life. But I didn't know what else to do so I stayed. Later on some people come and started digging through the rubble to find the bodies. I helped them. We found Mom and Dad. They laid them in a line with the others. I told the people they were my Mom and Dad. We didn't find Kazz. But there were a lot of bodies we didn't find.

After that I went away. I can't tell her where I went cos I don't know. Nor what I did. I just hung around.

I didn't want to live, I didn't want to die, I didn't want to do nothing nor nothing to ever happen again. But something did happen.

It was this girl. I was by the canal where it runs into the city. I seen her walking up the towpath towards me. I seen her from a long way off and watched her all the way till she come up to me. Then she stopped. I'd never seen her before but she knew who I was cos she said my name.

She said she'd been looking for me. If I went with her I'd see my sister. I asked her what my sister's name was. She told me. So I went with her. I followed down the canal till we come to where we are now. Ekt was here and the rest of the gang. There was a lot more then. And Kazz was here as well.

That's how I found her again, and that's how I come to be part of the gang. Though I ain't never really been part of it. I'm only here cos Kazz saved Ekt's life.

I tell her how I think it happened. What I can work out.

When the shelling started our street and all the streets around was hit. Most people was killed. Somehow Kazz wasn't. She was buried under the rubble but she found a way to crawl through. And while she was crawling through she must have found Ekt.

Ekt told me he'd been out with some of his gang and they got caught up in the shelling. They was running for cover when one of the shells landed on a house and it came down on top of them. He don't remember much after that. He says he come to once and it was dark and there was a weight crushing him and he couldn't breathe. Then he heard a voice talking to him, a girl's voice. He couldn't make out what she was saying but it made him feel better. The weight lifted off him and he could breathe again.

The next thing he remembers is waking up and he was outside and Kazz was with him. He reckons she must have found him down there and dragged him out. I reckon that's what must have happened as well. But we won't ever know for sure. The only one who knows is Kazz and she can't tell it so it makes sense.

Something happened to her down there to make her like she is. Something that nobody won't ever understand.

Sometimes, I say, the way she talks it's like she died and come back to life again. Like she found Ekt dead and brought him back to life as well.

I stop. I've finished telling her. She doesn't say anything for a long time.

Then she says, So that's it.

Yes, I say.

She doesn't say anything else. I don't want her to. Maybe she knows that. Or maybe she hasn't got anything to say.

They still haven't come. It must be early morning now. Can't be long before the sun rises. I look at the sky to see if it's getting light. It's still dark.

Mal's looking over at headquarters again.

I can't see them, she says.

Who? I say.

Nasty and Uba, she says. They're supposed to be guarding the entrance. I can't see them.

I look across. I can't see them either. But you can't see the entrance clear from here. It's all in shadow. I say that to her.

They'd better be there, she says.

They are, I say. One thing about them two, if they're told to do something they do it. Specially if Lex tells them. And Lex told them.

She seems a bit happier with that.

Look, she says.

She's pointing down the canal. There ain't so many buildings that way and you can see the sky where it meets with the ground. And as I look now I can see a faint edge of pale light running all along it.

Nearly morning, she says. It looks like we're going to be all right.

Yes, I say, it does. But it don't feel like that.

Then I say to her, Tell me something.

What? she says.

I want to know about Joey, I say.

What you want to know about him? she says.

How you met him, I say. Then I say, I told you about Kazz. Tell me about Joey.

She don't look at me.

I told you about Kazz and Ekt, I say. It sounds stupid when I've said it, like some little kid trying to get his own way, and I wish I hadn't.

Mal's looking at the light on the skyline.

All right, she says. I'll tell you.

She keeps looking at the light on the skyline.

Troggs: Nasty

Uba's chucking stones again.

He's always chucking stones. I asked him, why you always chucking stones, Uba, and he said to me, I ain't, and I said, yes, you am, you'm always chucking them, and he come back with, not always, so I come back to him with, not always but most of the time, so why'd you do it, why'd you keep chucking stones? He couldn't come back with nothing then, and he just shrugged and said, I don't know, I just like to, it's something I like to do. Well don't, I said, cos it gets on me nerves. And he stopped.

But now he's started up again. It ain't as if he's chucking them at anything. He's just chucking them. Lobbing them up into the air, and sometimes they fall far off and sometimes they fall close by and sometimes they fall and you don't know where cos you don't hear them. It's really pissing me off.

Uba, I say to him. That's really pissing me off.

What is, he says, and I say, that is, you chucking them stones, and he says, I ain't doing no harm, and I say, I'll be doing you some real harm in a minute if you don't give it a rest. He's got a stone in his hand ready to throw, and I see him looking down at it like he's going over something in his mind, which always takes Uba a long time. Then he looks up at me and tosses it up and catches it a couple of times. Then he drops it. He shrugs. It don't matter to me, he says. It's a big stone. He could've done some damage with it. Only Uba wouldn't think of doing nothing like that. Not unless somebody give him the idea.

I tell him to take a look in at Crowboy. He walks across to the door and pulls it open stoops down and looks inside. Then he straightens up and drops the door shut and comes back. He's just sitting, he says, like before. Just sitting. Head down, arms round his knees. That's what he was doing last time I looked in. And the time before that. That's what he's been doing ever since we put him in there. I pick up the stone that Uba dropped, take aim and chuck it good and hard. It flies across the canal and drops down by the scrap-heap. I hear it clatter.

What you doing, says Uba.

What's it look like, I says.

You chucked a stone, he says.

You'm right there, I says.

You had a go at me for chucking stones, he says.

I know, I says, want to make something of it, and I think for a minute maybe he does, and I'm going to have to sort him out, and I'm ready for that, all right, but he just says, no, I'm just saying, so I say, that's all right, then, and we leave it.

Shame though. I really feel like laying in to something, and he's the only thing around. I'm ready to bust wide open, and I can't do nothing about it, cos I'm stuck here looking after the loony, when what we should be doing is laying into the Geeks, getting in first and finishing them off, instead of waiting for them to come over here, which to me don't make no sense. It didn't make no sense when Ekt first told we and still don't make no sense now. I thought Lex was going to say something, I mean, he looked like he was, and I thought, yeah, there's gonna be trouble, a fight between Lex and Ekt, I seen it coming and I know whose side I'm on. But in the end he never said nothing. So here we am standing watch over that loony, which don't make no sense neither cos me and Uba we'm the two best fighters this gang's got and this puts we out of action. And what I really can't figure is it was Lex went along with that, and all.

And while I'm at it, the other thing is, he didn't look surprised when Ekt told we about finding Rok's body in the canal. Like he knowed it already. Knowed it was done, knowed who done it, or done it himself. So why ain't he said nothing about it? Why didn't he say nothing when Ekt told we his plan? Seems to me he's got some kind of plan of his own. If he has he ain't letting on. Not to me anyway.

It was a good throw anyway, says Uba, and for second or two I don't know what he's on about. Then I remember.

It wasn't so good, I say. I missed.

What was you aiming at, says Uba.

It don't matter, I say.

The thing about the loony we'm supposed to be guarding, I can't see what's so special about him. Except that he's a loony. But Kazz is a loony and all, ain't she, and there ain't nobody guarding her. I know I got all caught up in everything after the fight, shouting and cheering along with the rest of them. It was me lifted him up onto me shoulders and carried him around. But that was just the excitement of the fight, warn't it, the buzz of giving the Geeks a thrashing. It didn't mean nothing, and that loony don't mean nothing neither, so far as I can see. It wasn't no special power of his helped we beat the Geeks. It was we, we done it, and I don't see why he should get none of the glory. Nor none of this special treatment we'm giving him here. I'm starting to get really pissed off again.

Look. It's Uba speaking to me again. He's looking up into the sky.

What, I say.

Look up there, he says. I look. There ain't nothing to see, just the sky.

What am I looking at, I say to him.

How many you reckon there is, says Uba.

What you going on about, Uba, I say to him. How many what?

Them stars, he says.

Is that what we'm looking at, I say to him, and he says, yeah, and I say, what for, they'm just stars, and he goes on, but how many am there, and I say, I don't know, a lot, why don't you try counting them. Then he's quiet for a bit, and then he says, and who lives on them, you ever wondered that, and I say, no I ain't, cos there ain't nobody lives on them. A puzzled look comes on his face and he says, what they for then, and I say, what they for, they ain't for nothing, they just am, that's all.

He shakes his head. They must be for summat, he says, or why am they there. I mean, he says, like, everything's for summat, ain't it, I mean, it ain't for nothing, it can't be, cos if it was, like, you know, all of we and everything, like, I mean, it wouldn't, like.

I look at him a bit then I say, you got any idea what you'm going on about, and he says, no, but, and then he stops cos we both hear something. It's a stone, hitting the ground just a couple of feet away. Which means somebody chucked it, from down there at the far end of the warehouse. I walk over and pick it up.

It's one of them stones you was chucking, I say to Uba. Somebody's chucked it back. Uba don't find it funny. I look down the alley that runs between the warehouse and the factories, but I can't see nobody, which ain't a surprise cos it's all a jumble of shadows down there.

Who'd you reckon it is, he says.

Somebody playing silly buggers, I say.

You reckon it's them, he says.

Can't be, I say. They couldn't get across without we seeing them.

It must be somebody, he says, and I say, I know that, and he says, who is it, then, and I say, I don't know, and he says, well I'm going to find out. Then he says, give us that stone, so I give him the stone, and he takes it in one hand and picks up his weapon with the other and says, Right then, and walks off down the alley.

I watch him go till I can't see him no more then I wait. I wait a long time. Seems like a long time anyway. Still ain't nothing. I call out, Uba, but he don't answer. So now I'm certain, ain't I, summat's happened, and if summat happens you don't know what it is there's only one thing to do, ain't there, and that's go and find out. So I'm getting ready to do that when I hear the sound of footsteps and I see somebody down the alley coming towards me. That you, Uba, I say, but I can see it ain't, cos whoever it is ain't as tall as Uba, so I get a good grip on me weapon and make ready for what's coming.

But it's all right. It's Lex, coming towards me, grinning.

Lex, I say, you had me worried there. He don't say

nothing and stops, just a few feet away, still grinning, then he says, you ain't got nothing to worry about, and he comes towards me again just as I'm wondering where Uba is, and how Lex got over here without we seeing him and why he's soaking wet.

Troggs: Ik

So she tells me how she come to meet Joey.

Mal

It was when the soldiers broke into the city. My city. It had been under attack for a long time, but at last it fell, and the soldiers were in and they were everywhere. Burning, looting, killing. Terrible things were happening. People were running, just trying to get out. I was trying to get out as well, running, keeping my head down. I didn't know what had happened to my family. I'll tell you the truth, just then I didn't care. All I cared about was saving myself.

It was the same for everybody. People were just looking out for themselves. It was the only hope they had of staying alive.

At last I made it out of the centre. That's where the worst of it was going on. I was in the outskirts, not far from the city walls, and if I could make it there, I could find a way out, and I knew I'd be all right. It was a lot quieter where I was. Most of the houses had been empty for a long time, since the siege first started. A lot had been shelled flat. I stopped running, rested, caught my breath, then I carried on, just walking. The noise of the killing and the gunfire was a long way off.

I turned a corner by some half-fallen houses and came into a square where there was a church burning.

It was a small church and flames were coming out of its windows. I was across the other side of the square but I could feel the heat of the fire on my face. In the middle of the square, in between me and the church, there was a small group of soldiers. Four or five, not many. They didn't see me, but I could see their faces and they were laughing. Standing around like people at a bonfire party, talking and laughing. I couldn't hear their voices. Just the sound of the flames roaring as the church burned.

I took a few steps back. I was going to find some other way round the square. Then I heard something else and it stopped me. It was another sound coming from the church. Like it was part of the sound of the flames but separate from it as well. I tried to make out what it was. Then I recognized it. It was the sound of people screaming.

Men, women, children, screaming. Those soldiers standing around and laughing were burning people inside the church. They must have rounded them up and taken them in there. Or perhaps the people had gone in themselves for safety, and the soldiers had found them, and locked the doors, and set fire to the church. And now they were standing there waiting while they burned. Like it was just some job they had to do and get it over with.

I stood there too. I should've gone but I couldn't. I had to stay and watch and listen to the sound of the flames and the screaming until the screaming stopped and the roof of the church fell in and then there were just the flames and the light of the flames on the soldiers' grinning faces.

The soldiers were getting ready to go and I thought I'd better go too before they saw me, when suddenly there was somebody walking towards them. A boy. I didn't see where he came from, but he was walking away from the church. It was as if he'd come out of there, as if he was walking towards the soldiers out of the flames. But he couldn't have done, because he wasn't burned or anything. And he wasn't running, he was just walking slowly towards them. And he was carrying something in his arms.

I couldn't make out what it was at first. It looked like some kind of small bundle. But as he came closer to the soldiers, I saw. It was a child. Not much more than a baby. It was dead, lying loose in his arms. He carried this dead child out of the flames across the square to the soldiers and stopped and held it out towards them.

They stared at him. I suppose they couldn't believe what they were seeing, like I couldn't. One of them called out to him to stop but he didn't. They called out again, then they raised their rifles and pointed them at him and warned him not to come any closer or they'd shoot. But he kept on walking towards them. He walked right up to them and then he stopped.

He didn't say anything to them. He just stood there in front of them looking at them and holding out the dead child towards them.

I was waiting for them to shoot him. I was sure they would. But they didn't. They lowered their rifles and backed off. As if they were afraid of him. They backed off all the way to the edge of the square, then they turned and went away and left him there with the dead baby.

I went over to him. There wasn't anything else I could do. He was looking at the child in his arms. I stood in front of him, and he looked up at me like he expected me to be there. Then he spoke. He said we had to bury the baby. You couldn't tell if it had been a boy or a girl. It didn't even look human. Just something burned, something dead. We found a patch of bare ground among the rubble of the houses and dug a hole there with some pieces of slate and buried it.

The sun was going down. I wanted to get out of the city right then, but he sat on the ground by the grave and wouldn't move. And I couldn't leave him. Even though I knew I should be getting out, I couldn't leave him there on his own. I knew I had to stay with him. Like I was meant to stay with him. And I knew that I'd never leave him and that we were together now. So we stayed there together through the night. He didn't sleep, he didn't speak. He just sat there next to the grave. I slept a bit. When I woke up it was morning, the sun was just rising. He was standing up and he said it was time to go.

So we found a way out and left the city. At first I thought I was looking out for him, but after a while it seemed more like he was looking out for me. He led the way and I followed, and at last he led us all the way here.

Lex, Joey

Here you are, then. And here I am. Just the two of us together. Ain't nobody going to bother us. Got the whole place to ourselves. You. And me.

Can't see too good. Not much light. Just the fire burning in that old oil-drum over there. And it's nearly out. Maybe I should get it going again. Stoke it up. Get a better look at you. Why don't you lift your head? You know I'm here. Sitting right in front of you. Close enough to touch. Are you asleep? Maybe you think I'm some kind of bad dream you're having. When you wake you'll look up and I'll be gone. I got news for you. I ain't no dream. I'm real. I'm here. And I ain't going nowhere.

You ain't asleep. Come on. Stop playing games. Lift your head. Look up. Look at me. You ain't gonna win, not this game. I'm gonna sit here and wait till you look up. I'm stronger than you. I can wait for ever.

That's it. That's better. Now we can see each other. Face to face.

What is it about you? What's so special? You ain't nothing. Nothing special at all. Look at you. Just a skinny kid in rags. Should've called you Ragboy, not Crowboy. Like something the cat dragged in. Like something crawled into a hole and died. You don't fool me. I can see right through you. All the way through, right inside. And you know what I see? Nothing. There ain't nothing there. Just rags and tats. If I was to cut you open that's all would come falling out. Rags and tats, ashes and dust. Cos that's all you are. That's all you've ever been.

Got something to say about that? Eh? Well, have you? Thought you was going to say something then. Saw your lips move. What is it? What you got to say? Nothing.

I could do it now. There's nobody to stop me. Nobody outside to come and save you. I've seen to them. And you wouldn't stop me, would you? Wouldn't even try. You'd let me. Watch me take the knife out. Here. See it? Bring it towards you. Lift it, press it against your neck. Just a touch. You feel it? The point just there. It won't take much. A push. Then in. Slit your throat. Feel the blade go in, see the blood come out. Dark. A pool on the floor. That's all it takes. And there's nothing like it. After that you can do anything. You've crossed the line, and there's no stopping you. That's what they don't understand. The others. None of them. Once you've started you've got to keep going. No turning back. Go all the way.

And you're going to help me. Go all the way. How about that? You and me together. What a team.

So not yet. It's not time. That comes later. Take the knife away. See? No harm done. Just a little scratch. I bet you didn't even feel it.

Still nothing to say?

It's cold in here. That fire's out. Too late now. I'll have to leave you in the dark. Never mind. You'll be out of here soon.

They're on their way. Coming to get you. Have fun. See you around.

Joey

they're coming listen coming to get you fee
nowhere to run nowhere fi to hide they're coming
fo to get you fum ready or not feefifofum I smell
the blood of here we come one two three
    they take us inside you'll be safer in here out of the
way we'll look after you make sure you're all right smiles
on their faces they go out shut the doors we stand in the
dark some sit some kneel to pray I stand stone cool
under my feet I look at my feet standing on the cool stone
I don't look up I know he's there and I don't look up not
yet but I know I will I feel him there above me he wants
me to look but not yet then I look up I see him he's there
high above in the wall eyes of flame wings of flame a
burning sword in his hand he's not real mother said only
glass she said coloured glass mother said not real I know he
is he shines and the light burns through him and the light
is voices singing I hear them I look I keep on looking
through the light through the singing the voices and
there's a great noise and flames and somewhere screaming
and his wings my mouth's open I'm not screaming it's
somewhere else the screaming the great noise and the

*flames the roaring   and his wings are moving he's coming down   out of the window and here standing over me his wings around me somewhere else the roaring the screaming and he speaks I hear him speak he speaks out of the flames his voice   **do not fear   you shall not be harmed**   and his voice is thunder   **I am here to protect you to save you   you of all others   I shall save you and you shall save them**   he lifts his hands and in his hands is the offering   **take this as token to bear witness that they may know the fruits of their labours**   and I take it   the offering the token   **come with me   follow   I shall lead you to the place where it shall be made known**   his wings spread   rise about me   he walks into the flames I follow   through the flames and the roaring he leads me and the screaming and the thunder   and I follow*

here we come   one   two   three   GOT YOU!

Troggs: Ik

Some of what she's told me makes sense. Some of it doesn't. I want to ask her about it.

But she don't seem like she wants to be asked.

It's starting to get light now. Over by the headquarters the sky's turning grey. Soon it'll start to turn red and the sun will come up.

All night and they didn't come. That means more waiting around today. And maybe tonight. Or Ekt'll change his plan and we'll go across there to finish them off. Or get finished off ourselves.

I'm not waiting around for that.

I've got a plan.

We're going to get out of here. The four of us. Me, Mal, Joey, Kazz. Just take off and leave them to it.

First I got to get Ekt to put me and Mal on guard at the headquarters. Then I got to find a way of letting Kazz know what we're doing. Make sure she joins us. With the others spread around we should be able to get Joey out and then take off.

Sounds like a good plan.

Except Kazz could be a problem. Making her

understand. She don't always understand what you tell her. And she might not want to come. She might want to stay with Ekt.

If she does we'll have to go without her.

Then there's Lex. He'll know something's up. He's got a sense for things like that. We'll have to be careful.

But we got to try, got to give it a go. We got to get away from here. Things are bad. And they're going to get worse.

I never wanted to be part of all this anyway. Never wanted anything to do with any gangs. It just happened because of Kazz. But I never had a reason to go before. Nothing to go to. Now I've got a reason. And somebody to go with.

That's if she wants to. Only one way to find out.

I'm going to speak to her when suddenly she grips my arm.

Look, she says. She's staring towards the headquarters. I look.

With the light coming I can see that there's nobody on guard. But there is somebody coming across the lock-gate.

Joey, she says.

But it ain't Joey. It's Lex. Lex is coming across the lock-gate and now he's down the other side, and running towards the scrap-heap and he's shouting.

Geeks

'Got him!'
 'Hold him still.'
 'Make sure he don't get away.'
 'He won't get away.'
 'Put him over there.'
 'Let's take a look at him.'
 'See his face, yeah.'
 'Take the bag off his head.'
 'Careful, he might bite.'
 'If he does he won't have no teeth left.'
 'Ready, then?'
 'Yeah, go on.'
 'Right, here goes.'
 'Ain't much to look at.'
 'Nothing special.'
 'Looks dumb to me.'
 'Thought you said he was summat special.'
 'I didn't say it. It's what Lex said.'
 'Got some kind of power, has he?'
 'I dunno, ask him.'
 'Hey, you, you got some kind of magic power?'

'You a wizard?'

'A super-hero?'

'A secret weapon?'

'He might be a human bomb!'

'Stand back in case he goes off.'

'Smells to me like he's gone off already.'

'He's pissed himself!'

'Disgusting!'

'Revolting.'

'Ain't much, is he?'

'Don't say much, neither.'

'I'll get some noise out of him.'

'Not a squeak.'

'Hit him harder.'

'Still nothing.'

'Perhaps he can't feel nothing.'

'He felt that, all right.'

'And that.'

'Bleeds like the rest of we, and all.'

'Want more of that?'

'You better start talking.'

'Who are you?'

'What's your name?'

'Where you come from?'

'What you doing here?'

'It's here.'

'What?'

'What did he say?'

'It's here.'

'What's here?'

'Here now with wings and flame and a great wind rises and a thunder—'

'What's he going on about?'

'—and out of the wind and thunder comes the flame—'

'Eh?'

'—and out of the flame comes the burning and the light and all shall go into the burning all shall go into the light—'

'You what?'

'—and all shall be scattered all shall be gathered all shall be broken all shall be mended—'

'Give it a rest.'

'—and all shall be one but first comes the flame.'

'Has he finished?'

'Wish he'd never started.'

'What was that all about, then?'

'What's it all mean?'

'Nothing. It don't mean nothing.'

'Yeah. It don't mean nothing. He ain't nothing.'

'Whatever Lex told you he was talking through his arse.'

'Just a dummy.'

'Let's do him.'

'Do him over, yeah.'

'Do him good and proper.'

'Let's do him like they done Rok.'

'You mean it?'

'I mean it.'

'Really do him?'

'Do him in.'

'They done it to one of ours.'

'We'll do it to one of theirs.'

'It's only right.'

'It's only fair.'

'Do it to them like they done it to us.'

'Blood for blood.'

'An eye for an eye.'

'Yeah. That's it. Summat like that.'

Cgeeks: Schyte

Jax is holding him one side and Dis the other and Little
Jax is dancing around getting himself all worked up and
excited, Woo, yeah, go on, yeah, go on, he's saying, and
Fig's in front of me so's I can't see her face but I can see
her's got her fists clenched all tight and Akh's standing
in front of him and you can tell from his face he means
it. The others am all for it, and all, but me, I ain't so
sure, I mean it's one thing to give somebody a good
going over, ain't it, I'm all for that, but doing somebody
in's summat else, even if they done it don't mean we
have to. It ain't even like he's one of them just some
crazy kid don't look like he knows where he is nor who
he is probably nor what's going on, just standing there,
they don't even have to hold him, he ain't no harm to
nobody, but what can I do about it, it's just me, ain't it,
ain't nobody can stop Akh doing something's he's set
himself to, I'd get just the same if I tried, so what's the
point, there ain't nothing I can do. Little Jax is still
dancing around, Wow, woo, yeah, yeah, then Akh says
Shut up, and he shuts up and stands still, and his eyes
am staring at him, everybody's eyes am staring at him,

mine and all, like there ain't nobody else in the world and suddenly it's all quiet, and you can feel it coming. Me throat's dry and me legs am trembling all weak like they'm going to give way, and I got this fluttering in me guts and a kind of buzzing noise in me head coming from far away closer and closer, and I'm thinking it ain't going to happen, he ain't going to do it, then I see him, Akh, I see him lift the crowbar he's got in his hand, and this is it now, I don't want to look but I got to keep looking, he lifts it right up above his head, then somebody says Hold it, and we all turn round.

It's Ekt what spoke. There he is with the others, Lex and Ell and Yass and Kazz and that girl, but Nasty and Uba ain't there, I wonder what's happened to them, and they got weapons with them, except for Kazz, her's hanging back, her never takes part, so it looks like we'm in for a fight, and I'm glad of that cos that's the kind of trouble I can deal with, and Akh says, What you doing over here, and Ekt says, You know what, we've come for him, and Akh says, You can have him back soon as I've done with him. Ekt takes a step forward then and says, You ain't going to do it, Akh, he says, and Akh says, Ain't I, just wait and see, he's gonna pay for what you done to Rok, and Ekt comes back with, We already paid for that, and twice over, he says, and Akh says, You ain't paid for nothing yet, then Ekt starts going on about how we killed two of theirs when we come and took the Crowboy, and I reckon it must be Nasty and Uba he's talking about and that's why they ain't there, but it don't make no sense to me cos we didn't kill nobody, we just went across there through the tunnel I found and took him from their headquarters, we didn't see nobody there to kill, and I remember thinking then how it was funny them putting nobody to guard him seeing as how they reckoned he was so special and all.

So they'm going on arguing backwards and forwards, stuff like, You want him, you try and take him, from Akh, and That's what we come here for, from Ekt, and I'm getting ready for Akh to give the word and the first one I'm going for is that girl, but all of a sudden Ekt's saying summat about single combat, him and Akh, just the two of them. It ain't about the Crowboy, says Ekt, it ain't even about Rok, you know that, it's about me and you. And Akh says, I reckon you'm right there, it's been a long time coming, and Ekt says, It has, so let's have it settled here and now. So that's what they're going to do, fight it out, and whoever wins leads both gangs, so there won't be two gangs no more, just one like there used to be. Then we all have to give our word to go along with it, whatever happens, and we spit on our hands and say pax, then stand back and make room, and Ekt and Akh face up, and they're all set.

First off there ain't neither of them make a move, just standing there staring each other out, then circling round, looking for a way in. Akh's got his crowbar, and he's keeping it low, opening himself up like he's daring

Ekt to have a go, which I can see he wants to, cos he's holding his weapon up and at the ready, a nasty-looking axe it is with its blade all chipped and none too sharp, but he can still do some damage with it. He ain't daft, though he knows Akh is trying to draw him in, and he ain't sure he wants to go just yet. But the way his legs am bent and his body's leaning forward all tense you can tell he's just dying to get in there, thinking to himself, Maybe I'll be lucky, maybe catch him off his guard, have it all over and done with before he knows what's hit him. And that's just what he does, ain't it, he makes a move and he's in there quick, but of course Akh's ready for him and quicker, he blocks him, and swings round and Ekt goes stumbling forward and looking round like to say, Where's he gone, behind you, that's where, and he's swinging his crowbar into Ekt's back, and swinging it again, and down he goes, and here comes Akh for number three, but Ekt's round and thumping his axe into Akh's gut, which gives him time to get up onto his feet, then they're both in there and at it, slogging away, and each of them giving as good as he gets.

By this time we'm all shouting, them for theirs and we for ours, and you can't tell which way it's going to go, they're both giving it out and taking it hard, when all of a sudden I don't know how it happens but Akh swings at Ekt and misses, he can't see proper cos of the blood in his eyes, and he stumbles kind of, misses his footing, and Ekt does just what I'd do, he's right in there with the back of his axe crack on the side of Akh's head, you can hear the noise, and Akh's down, dropping his crowbar, and falling so heavy you can see he ain't getting up again. Then we all stop shouting, them and us, and it goes quiet, and there's Akh on his hands and knees, and there's Ekt standing over him looking down. He's breathing heavy, the axe hanging from his hand like he ain't got the strength to lift it, but he does, he takes it in both hands and lifts it up above his head, and we'm all just waiting now, cos it looks like there's only one way this is going to end.

Joey

this is the place   yes   *where it shall be known*   now
here he is here now   he speaks inside me   *all shall*
see me shining in human form   he and I when he
speaks I speak   *take this token to bear witness*   I am
his voice his human form   *that they may know the*
fruits of their labours   I am the token   *I shall save you*
the offering   *and you shall save them*   that they shall
see it shall be known and he and I and I shall save and
here and now

   yes

Mal

And then Joey's there.

The two who were holding him must have loosed him when the fight started. I suppose they forgot about him. I forgot about him myself, shouting along with the others, falling quiet and watching as Ekt raised the axe. But now he's there, walking into the circle, towards Ekt. He's holding his arms out in front of him, and I think of when I first saw him, walking out of the burning church, carrying the dead child towards the soldiers.

He stops in front of Ekt and looks at him. Then he speaks. Just two words, clear and sharp-edged.

'No more.'

His voice is quiet but we all hear him. The sound of it cuts through the cold of the early morning. As if he's speaking it to all of us. But his eyes are fixed on Ekt. He stands there, staring at him, and there's a look on his face, I can't describe it, but I think again of him standing in front of the soldiers, because that's when I saw that same look. And it goes straight through Ekt, buries itself deep inside him. And like the soldiers Ekt backs off, and he lowers the axe.

And suddenly it becomes clear to me. This is what it's for. This is the reason we came here. He was leading us to this place, this moment. To stop the killing. So there won't be any more dead children. And he didn't know it himself, not until now.

Now Ekt holds the axe out to Joey, and lays it in his hands. Joey's fingers close around the handle, and Ekt lets it go. He watches what happens as if he can't quite believe it, and then there's a look of relief on his face, like somebody waking up out of a bad dream. He looks at his hand that's not holding the axe any more and he's glad. Glad that Joey stopped him, that he hasn't got to go through with what it was he was going to do. Joey's taken it from him. I don't know what's going to happen now, and neither does Ekt, but it doesn't matter. Everything's changed, everything's different, nothing will be the same again.

Nobody says anything. Nobody moves. We can all feel the change that's happened. Feel ourselves changing with it.

The sun's coming up. Its light falls on Joey's face, on all our faces.

Then Ekt walks over to Akh. Akh looks up, like he's waiting for Ekt to raise the axe, bring it down and finish him off. But Ekt doesn't have the axe any more, and he holds out his empty hand towards Akh. Akh looks at the hand, looks up at Ekt, and there's a puzzled look on his face, like he doesn't understand why he's still alive, or what it is that Ekt's doing. Ekt doesn't say anything. He just stands there with his hand outstretched.

And still with that puzzled look Akh reaches up to take hold of it.

But suddenly Lex runs forward. He pushes past Joey, grabs Ekt, pulls him away, knocks him down. Now he's standing over Akh and he's raising his arm above his head. There's something in his hand. It's the axe.

Everything's still and quiet. Frozen. Like looking at a picture of something that happened a long time ago. Then Ekt shouts out.

'Lex! What you doing?'

Lex answers without looking at him.

'What you should've done. Only you didn't have the guts.'

Akh's looking up at Lex, still with his arm raised from when he was going to take hold of Ekt's hand. Still with that puzzled look on his face. But just then the look on his face changes. He's not puzzled any more, he knows what's going on. And in that moment of knowing, Lex drops his arms and brings the axe down on top of his head.

And now things look like they're coming apart, the picture's starting to break up, splintering like the glass in the burning church. Separate images that don't mean anything. There's the axe falling from Lex's hand. Akh falling back slowly onto the ground. Ekt rising to his feet, stumbling backwards. A pool of dark blood spreading outwards. Joey with his mouth open and no sound coming out.

Then there's a cry, a long wailing howl, coming from far off, and it's that cry that holds everything together, stops the pieces from breaking up. It's getting closer, becoming a scream that pierces everything like a spike, and fixes it all in place. It fixes Joey, with his mouth still open, and his arms stretched out towards Akh, as if somehow he can help him. And I want to run to Joey, do something, I don't know what, but I can't, because I'm fixed here too by that scream, unable to move.

Then the scream stops and there's silence again.

Suddenly there's a voice.

'It's over!'

It's Lex. His voice hard, smashing through the silence like the axe-blade.

'Akh's dead. Ekt couldn't finish him so I did. I'm leader now. And there ain't no more Geeks, no more Troggs. Just one gang, like there used to be. We'll start again, be better than we ever was. The best gang in the city. The only gang in the city. Anybody don't agree?'

He looks round at us all. Nobody says anything.

'Right,' he says. 'And the first thing is to get rid of anybody who ain't one of us.'

He points at Joey, and there's a knife in his hand.

'And we'll start with him.'

The screaming starts again, coming faster now, getting

closer and louder. I can't tell if it's inside me, or outside, or both. And then there's another sound, rising out of the screaming, a thin sound, a voice trying to be heard. At the same time as I hear it I feel it tearing its way out of my throat, my voice, crying out, 'No!'

Lex swings round towards me, the knife still raised in his hand. I shout at Lex, at the knife.

'You can't do this! He came to stop it! You can't!'

He grins.

'Watch me,' he says. Then he raises his voice and speaks to the others.

'And her. She ain't one of us neither. And she's the one who killed Rok.'

Somebody grabs me by the arm and I turn, lifting my weapon to strike, but it's Ik, and he's saying to me, 'Run, take off, now. You might just make it. Go on!'

I just stare at him and he says again, like he knows what's in my head, 'You can't help him. Ain't nothing can. Save yourself. But you got to go now.'

And suddenly that's what I want to do. Make a break for it, run, save myself. But I want to run the other way, too, towards Joey, try and save him. And I can't do both. And I don't get the chance to do either. Because just then somebody takes hold of me from behind, a hand round my neck, another twisting my arm behind my back, and I'm dragged into the circle, next to Joey and Lex. I struggle, but whoever's holding me is strong and I can't get free. A fist thumps me in the stomach.

I double up, sick, gasping for breath. At the same time I hear Ik.

'This ain't right, Lex!'

And Lex calls back, 'You're next, Ik. And your crazy sister. You was never part of the gang. There ain't no room for you. We're making a fresh start.'

I raise myself up. Fingers are biting into my arms. It's no good trying to break free, I know that. I'll be held here like this until Lex kills me. In a way I don't care any more. I feel past all that. All I want to do now is speak to Joey.

His face is a few inches from mine, looking away from me. I want him to turn and look at me. I want to see what's in his eyes. Maybe there'll be something there to explain all this. Why everything went wrong. I say his name but he doesn't seem to hear me. It's because of the screaming, it's here, now, all around, inside me. But I have to make him hear, make him turn his head. If only the screaming would stop, just long enough for him to hear me say his name, and look at me.

Then suddenly it does.

There's silence.

And everything explodes in flame.

The ground heaves, throwing me up into the air, and I come down heavily on top of someone. We struggle together, then I'm pushed off, and a voice cries out, 'They're shelling the city!'

And another, 'Take cover!'

The ground shakes again, and again, there's another explosion, a burst of flame, a cloud of dust rising. Through the cloud I can see shadowy figures running, stumbling, falling over, getting up and running again. The only two who aren't running are Lex and Joey. They're standing just where they were before the shelling started. A figure appears out of the dust above me and says, 'Get up! Come on! Get out of here!'

I think it's Ik, but I can't be sure because just then there's another explosion and when the dust from that clears a little he's gone.

But Lex and Joey are still there. Lex has his knife raised. I try to get up but my legs give way and I fall back again. I watch as Lex makes a move towards Joey, then stops. I see what it is that's made him stop. Joey's lifting his arms, opening them, reaching out towards Lex. And he's smiling. Lex stares at Joey. He lowers his knife. Joey steps towards him.

Then there's a great roaring of wind and the dust clears and the sky opens in a burst of fire and light, and the wind picks me up and flings me into the flame.

Ik, Kazz

It's over.

Everything's quiet now. I think the soldiers must be moving out. The shooting's stopped. It went on all yesterday and all last night. Just before dark a few soldiers came down here. We hid and they looked around for a bit then went away. We haven't seen anybody else. There isn't anybody else left.

Just me and Mal and Kazz.

I don't know how we come through it. I don't remember much. Coming to and thinking I was dead and buried. Realizing I wasn't dead but I was in the bottom of a hole half-buried under a pile of bricks. Crawling out, stumbling around, choking on the dust. Then seeing Mal, and the two of us finding Kazz, but not finding anybody else.

And not finding Joey.

We looked a long time for him, till it started to get dark, then we give up.

It's starting to get light. Up there I can see the black smoke rising from the centre. Must be fires burning everywhere, and nobody to put them out. They'll

221

probably burn for days. Burn until there's nothing left. By that time we'll be gone. We're moving out soon as it's lighter. There ain't nothing to stay for.

That's what I said anyway. Mal just nodded.

Yeah, OK, she said.

Then she got up and walked away.

Kazz didn't say anything.

She hasn't said anything since it happened. She just sits there. She's sitting there now, on a pile of rubble, winding her fingers together, over and over, like she's trying to undo some kind of knot or tangle. Staring at her fingers, winding and unwinding them.

I go across to Mal. She's standing where the scrap-heap used to be. There's just a hole there now. A shell must've dropped right on top of it. One dropped on the headquarters as well. What's left of it is in the canal.

I was looking for something to take with us, she says. I thought I might find something. A piece of that figure he made. But there's nothing.

We could stay a bit longer, I say. Look for him. Keep looking till we find him.

She shakes her head.

He's not here, she says. He's gone.

I look around. I don't recognize anything, except the canal, and that's full of rubble. The lock-gate's smashed. Most of the old factory buildings are gone, and a lot of the houses. It's just open wasteland. She's right. If he was here, alive or dead, we'd have found him by now.

So we'd best go, she says. And soon.

I'll tell Kazz, I say.

I start to walk over to Kazz. She's still on the pile of rubble but her fingers have stopped moving and she's not looking at them any more.

Something's coming up out of the canal, a figure climbing over the side, covered in filth and dust. It drags itself up onto the bank and crouches there on all fours, coughing, spitting. Then it raises its head, stands up and looks at us.

Joey, I say.

But it's not Joey. It's Schyte.

He comes towards us, walking funny, staggering and shuffling from side to side like he don't know how to walk straight. He's talking, but I can't make out what he's saying. It's just words tumbling out of his mouth, jumbled up together and no sense to them.

Flying through the air don't know if it's me head or me arse then it all comes down on top of me whump and I might've got drownded only the water's gone so I'm digging and the next thing here I am and you'm here and all and I can't walk straight . . .

Shut up, Schyte, I say.

He shuts up.

Then I ask him, Where you been?

That's what I'm telling you, he says. In the canal, only

you can't say it's a canal no more cos there ain't no water in it, just bricks and rubble, and that's where I was, under all the rubble, and I been all this time digging me way out, I've gone dizzy, I got to sit down.

And he drops down and sits there for a bit breathing deep and shaking his head. Mal comes across.

Where did he come from, she says.

I tell her.

Schyte looks up.

You're here and all, he says. Any more of you?

No, I say. We thought it was just us till you turned up.

There might be some more turn up then, he says.

I don't reckon so, I say. We looked everywhere else. The only place we didn't look was the canal.

I wish you had, he says, you might've saved me a bit of bother.

Or might just've left you there, I say.

You wouldn't've done that, he says.

Kazz is trying to undo that knot with her fingers again. Schyte watches her.

What's she doing, he says.

I shake my head. He looks away, up along the canal to where the black smoke's rising in the distance.

We ought to find something to eat, he says.

We're getting out, I say.

Ain't nothing to stay for, he says. Where you going?

I don't know, I say.

He stands up.

I'll come with you, he says, let me come with you, you'll need somebody like me, somebody who knows how to get on, I mean you ain't gonna make it very far, just the three of you, you'll make it a lot further if I'm with you, and I know a good way out.

I ask him what is it. He tells me there's a tunnel under the canal, it leads outside the city. He says there might be some food down there as well.

Then Mal speaks.

It's where we came in, she says. Me and Joey.

Who's Joey, says Schyte.

The Crowboy, I say.

The old man showed us. He didn't want to. He said we should keep out of the city. He said it was bad and things were going to get worse. I knew he was right. But Joey said we had to come in, so we did. Through that tunnel. But I can't remember where it is.

I can, says Schyte.

Show us, then, I say. You might as well come along.

I squat down next to Kazz, take hold of her hands, stop her winding her fingers together. She looks at me sudden. I ain't sure she knows who I am. I tell her we're leaving.

It's time to go, I say. Come on, Kazz.

I help her to her feet. We're ready to make a start. But Schyte hangs back. He stands looking across the wasteland that used to be our territory and theirs. All

laid flat now by the shelling, and you can't tell where
ours ended and theirs began.

It warn't right, he says, what we done. Taking him. It
seemed like it was right, but when I seen him, I knowed
it warn't. I di'n't want no part of it then. But there
wasn't nothing I could do.

Then he looks at us and he says, There warn't no
harm in him.

He tried to show us something, says Mal. When he
took the axe away from Ekt. When he stopped him
from killing Akh. It's what he came for. To show us
that.

He didn't stop Lex, says Schyte.

Mal turns to him.

It wasn't Lex who killed Akh, she says. It was us. All
of us. We let it happen. We let him down.

She looks away.

Maybe next time we won't, she says.

Next time? I say.

She's going to say something, but it's Kazz who
speaks instead. It's the first time she's spoke since it
happened.

He went into the fire. I saw. He was there and the fire
came. There was a wind and there was a roaring but
there was no harm. A brightness and a shining. He
opened his arms and they were wings. Wings of flame,
wings of light, and they rose about him, and he was gone.
Into the brightness and the shining.

Then lifts up her hand. She's holding something in it, between her fingers. Black, ragged, shiny. A feather.

And we shall follow.

She looks at me. The brightness, the shining. The war. I know where we're gonna be going now.

Orf

So I'm standing that morning outside what's left of the city, watching the sun coming up over the hills, and wondering if I should take anything else with me, and maybe I should go back inside for a last look round. But I reckon I've seen enough of what's laying around there, it ain't a pretty sight, and not one you want to become too acquainted with if you're going to sleep any way easy. Besides, I've already got enough on me back, and I want to get a move on. I ain't following the war, though, not this time. I've decided I'm getting too old for that lark. I can see which way it's heading, the cloud of dust rising around it out there in the distance, and I'm heading in the opposite direction. I want to find meself somewhere peaceful to rest up and see me days out. Somewhere I can sleep a bit more easy. So I'm just hitching me pack up a bit higher and I'm about to take the first step, and that's when I see them.

They're walking out across the ruins, four of them, two girls and two boys, scrawny and scraggy-looking, and it takes me a bit by surprise, cos I reckoned as how I was the only one come out of that alive, though it looks to me like they'm hardly living, more like ghosts just got up out of the grave. And as they get a bit closer I recognize one of them, that kid as I caught in me hideaway the night before the shelling started. And he recognizes me and all, and gives me a grin, and comes across, and says to me, 'You got a lot on your back there, mate, how about giving us some to carry for you?'

'Still on the scrounge, then,' I say to him.

'You know me,' he says, 'I'm always on the scrounge.'

'You still got them boots I give you,' I say.

'Yeah,' he says, 'and they'm still too small.'

'I'll take them back, if you like,' I say.

'No,' he says. 'I reckon I'll keep them. How about it, then, you got any food?'

So I take me pack off me back and set it down, open it up and take out a few tins of something or other and lay them out on the ground. I give them an opener as well cos of course they don't have one and I've got a spare. Last of all I give them one of my plastic bottles to put some water in. Then I fasten me pack and hitch it up onto me back again, while they share out the cans between them.

'That should keep you going for a bit,' I say.

'Long enough,' says one of the girls, and it's only then when I take a look that I recognize her.

'You made it out, then,' I say.

'Looks like it,' she says.

I look at the other two, the other boy and girl, both of them small with dark hair. I haven't seen them before. The boy's putting some of the cans into his pocket, and then holding out the plastic bottle to the girl. She looks at him like she doesn't understand what he wants her to do. He takes her hands and puts them around the bottle, but she drops it, and he picks it up and carries it himself.

'What about the one who was with you?' I say. 'The boy. What was his name?'

'Joey,' she says.

'That's it,' I say. 'Joey.'

I remember him standing in front of me, holding a piece of wire in his hands, and I remember his voice, almost like I can hear it, like I can see him there now.

'It was a bird in a cage. But now the cage is broken and the bird's free.'

I shake my head.

'What happened to him?' I ask her.

'He's gone,' she says, and I think I know what she means, but she says it in a way that it might mean something else. 'It's a long story,' she says.

'You owe me a story,' I say. 'Remember?'

'Come with us and I'll tell it to you,' she says.

'Where you heading?' I ask her.

She nods towards the cloud of dust.

'I'd have thought you'd had enough of that,' I say to her, and she doesn't say anything, just shrugs, and the one who's wearing me boots says, 'It's where the action is, ain't it?'

'If that's what you're after,' I say, 'but I ain't.'

Then the girl says, 'I thought you followed the war,' and I tell her I used to, but not no more, and if they was heading in that direction, I was heading in the other.

'You'll have to have that story some other time, then,' she says.

'Yes,' I say, 'some other time.'

They're starting to move off now, and as they pass me, the other girl, the dark one, she says something, and I can't tell whether it's to me or to herself, her voice is so soft and low.

'He goes before us.'

I don't know if I've heard her right, and if I have what it means, and I don't reckon I want to find out neither cos I've a feeling it'd just make me feel worse about them than I already do. Some things it's best just not to know.

The sun's up and I watch them walking out onto the plain, following that cloud of dust way off on the horizon, four kids, they've been through it, and where they're going they look set to go through it again, and worse before they're done, and the oldest can't be any more than fourteen. The sky's clear and cold above them, and the light so sharp it gives a kind of flicker, like a twist of flame above their heads, and it hurts my eyes and I have to look away for a minute. When I look again they're further off, fading into that light. Then I find meself wondering, well maybe I should go with them, it ain't going to be easy, and they could do with somebody to look out for them.

And I would like to hear that story.

Course, the best thing I could do for meself is turn round and head off in the opposite direction. There's all kinds of trouble waiting for them out that way, and for me if I go with them, and I'm getting too old for that game. If they want to go chasing the war, let them get on with it, I got me own life to live, what there is left of it, and I could do without the bother. And they're so far off now it'll take me a while to catch up with them if I ever do.

And even as I'm thinking all that I hitch me pack a bit higher on me back and follow the way they're going.